Charlie's Run

Charlie's Run

VALERIE HOBBS

FRANCES FOSTER BOOKS

FARRAR STRAUS GIROUX   NEW YORK

Distributed in Canada by Douglas & McIntyre, Ltd.
Printed in the United States of America
Designed by Rebecca A. Smith
First edition, 2000

Library of Congress Cataloging-in-Publication Data
Hobbs, Valerie.
    Charlie's run / Valerie Hobbs. — 1st ed.
        p.   cm.
    Summary: Hoping to stop his parents' impending separation and keep them
from getting a divorce, eleven-year-old Charlie runs away from their house in the
California countryside and finds a ride to the coast.
    ISBN 0-374-34994-0
    [1. Runaways—Fiction.   2. Divorce—Fiction.   3. California—Fiction.]
    I. Title.
    PZ7.H65237Ch   2000
    [Fic]—dc21   99-22376

FOR ALLAN

Charlie's Run

1

Charlie Bascomb felt words. He felt them in the way some people felt cold or heat. There were words that could make him feel good, no matter what was happening in his family. All he had to do was say them in his mind. *Blueberry, swoon, scalawag, sylvan, sympathy, lullaby, luminous* . . .

There were plenty of awful words, too, of course and Charlie felt them as well. He couldn't help it. Words like *squander, deodorant, pusillanimous, cadaver, lurid, numskull, obliterate, smug,* and *spite.* But the worst word was one nobody said, a word that just lurked in the bushes like a great yellow-eyed tiger waiting to pounce. His father wouldn't say the word at the dinner table tonight and neither would his mother but it was there all the same.

"Separate," they said instead. "A little break."

Charlie could tell that his mother was trying not to

cry, but her eyes were red as a rabbit's. Her nervous fingers kept reaching for things on the table and putting them down again. His father was wearing his stone face. He was explaining very carefully how things had been arranged so that nothing would change in the children's lives. They would live in the same old house they had always lived in, with their three dogs, seven cats, all the fish, and Molly the horse. Nothing would change, their father said this several times with his forehead all scrunched up. Nothing would change.

Which could never in a million years be true. Charlie knew what happened when families split up. It had happened to his friends, Mark and Tony, and to Mark's cousin, Lisa, all in one school year. The fathers disappeared. Poof. Gone. The ones who stuck around—some of them did, Tony's father for one—showed up on weekends acting weird, spoiling their kids in ways they never would if they were full-time fathers. Did his dad really believe that nothing would change? Did he think he and Tom and Carrie didn't *know*?

Nobody said anything after the big announcement, not Charlie, not his brother or sister. They just sat there looking at Mom and Dad, listening to Pager scratch and whine at the door to be let in. Then Tom, the oldest, cleared his throat as if he had something to say, but nothing came out. He scratched his head real hard, back and forth through his spiky hair. Carrie let out a little scream-cry, pushed herself back from the table, and ran out of the room. "Carrie, honey—!" cried Charlie's mother, but they all sat still and listened as Carrie thundered up the stairs and slammed the door to her room. Carrie was in a "difficult period," their mother said. But Carrie had always been in a difficult period. She was never out of one. Carrie was just difficult. Period.

Wesley was oblivious—that was one of Charlie's final spelling words from sixth grade. Not a bad word or a good word, just an interesting word. Wesley kept sticking pieces of food into his mouth with his sticky baby fingers, kernels of corn and shriveled peas. He was only two and looked the most like Charlie, with coarse brown hair that went its own way and big blue eyes. Charlie hoped Wesley wouldn't have to wear glasses when he got bigger, the thick kind that made Charlie's blue eyes look as if he was always staring. But if he did, well, there were worse things. Charlie knew that now.

"Tom?" their father said. Tom looked up from his empty plate, where he'd smeared bread through his gravy to make gnarly-looking waves. Charlie couldn't tell at first whether Tom was mad or sad, but then Tom said real loud in his deep voice, "I think it *sucks*. It doesn't matter what you say, things are going to be different and you know it. We're *broken*," he said, his eyes wide and crazy. "We're a broken family now. Just another damned statistic. You make me sick!" Then he, too, got up and left with long angry strides heading toward the back door. The screen screeched, then slammed behind him, and Pager came in, wagging her back end. When she stuffed her cold nose into Charlie's hand he felt like crying, like bursting right out and crying. But he didn't.

"Charlie? You all right, sweetie?" His mother blew her nose into her own paper napkin and then into his father's. In his mind, Charlie said the word, the worst word in the world, to try it out. *Divorce*, he heard his mind say, *divorce*. "Charlie?" Charlie shrugged. He didn't know what to say. He didn't even know what to feel. It was like the time he ran his skateboard into the tailgate of his father's pickup and knocked himself out for a minute. Like after-an-accident numb.

His mother got up and came around the table and hugged his head, knocking his glasses crooked, but Charlie let them be. He closed his eyes and let his right ear and his cheek rest against her warm belly and thought for a minute that maybe it was going to be all right. But when he opened his eyes again and saw the mess on the table, he knew it wasn't.

"There's a swimming pool at my condo," his father said. "You can come every weekend if you want. You and Carrie . . . Tom . . ." All of a sudden his father looked strange, as if he'd gotten lost somehow in a dark place and couldn't find his way back out. Charlie felt sorry for his father, who wouldn't be living in the house anymore. He felt sorry for Tom and for Carrie, and Wesley, who didn't know peas from corn. He felt sort of sorry for himself, too, but he didn't think he was supposed to do that, so he tried to stop. He didn't get all worked up about things the way Tom and Carrie did. When Tom blew his cool or Carrie whined or the two of them fought over who got the biggest slice of pizza, Charlie just hung back and watched. Then he jumped in and tried to make things right again. That was his job. "My little Mister Sunshine," his mother had said a long time ago, when he was in kindergarten. He never forgot it.

He watched his mother blow her nose, one last hard time. He watched her wet a washcloth and grab for Wesley, who started squirming and yelling the minute water touched his face. He watched his father get up and go out the back door. The screen screeched, but this time his father didn't say, "I'm going to get to that one of these days." Now Charlie knew that one of these days was never going to come. His mother hoisted Wesley with his big fat legs up into her arms and went out the other door, toward the kids' rooms.

That left Charlie.

He sat at the empty table looking at six dirty dinner plates. When they were clean they were white with a dark blue band around them, and they'd been around as long as he had. At least. But now they looked weird for some reason. Like they weren't his family's dishes but somebody else's, some other family's. Charlie sat at the empty table and wondered what would happen when his father wasn't sitting at one end anymore. Would they still leave a space for him? Would his chair still be there?

Blueberry, swoon, scalawag, sylvan . . .

2

Charlie wandered into the den, where he had the "dog couch" all to himself. *Star Trek* was on the TV. If this had been an ordinary day, it would have been good to have the whole couch, dog hair and all. Now only one of his ears listened to the TV. The other listened for the screen door, for Tom or his dad to come back in. He heard Wesley squealing in the bedroom, but nothing from upstairs, where Carrie was probably on the telephone to Dodi Walsh or Tony's sister, who was also named Carrie.

Captain Picard was having a problem with Data, who was acting like a human again. It was getting so bad they were going to have to lock him in a room until he recovered. No matter how bad things got on the *Enterprise*, nobody said the worst word. Nobody moved out. Of course it helped to be in deep space. You couldn't exactly open the back door and leave.

Captain Picard was a problem-solver. That's what a captain was. Charlie's mind kept shifting between the TV and his own real family. There had to be a way to make this all go away. Before someone said the most terrible word and they were a broken family for good. Somebody had to make their mother and father change their minds. "There isn't a darned thing you can't get done," his father always said, "if you set your mind to it."

He went upstairs and knocked on Carrie's bedroom door. First a little testing knock. Then, when she didn't answer, a loud one. Carrie opened the door and stuck her head out. Her pink telephone was attached to her head like an octopus. "What do you want? I'm on the phone." Carrie's eyes were red and puffy. She looked angry, as if her face would explode. Charlie shrugged and backed off. Downstairs, he'd had a half-cooked idea that he and Carrie could do something together, could make a plan, something to make their parents change their minds. Now he didn't know what to say to his sister with her angry face. He clumped back down the stairs.

In the den the TV was turned off and his mother was reading Wesley a story about fireflies. Wesley just wanted the pages to turn faster. His mother looked up and smiled a weary, sad smile. "We forgot the dessert," she said. "Carrot cake. It's in the refrigerator."

"Okay," Charlie said.

"Go ahead and have some," his mother said to the book. "*The firefly saw a light and flew toward it . . .*"

"Fwy," said Wesley, pointing his fat baby finger in the air.

"Okay," Charlie said. But he went past the refrigerator and out the squeaking back door. The garage light was on, so he figured his father was out there tinkering with the car Tom would get on his sixteenth birthday. Tom and Dad worked on the car together and sometimes they let Charlie help, hand them the right wrenches and stuff. Charlie didn't think Tom would be working on the car tonight. He probably walked all the way to Four Corners instead to call one of his friends.

Tom wouldn't have made a good *Enterprise* captain. He just got mad when things didn't work right with the engine. He'd give up, throw a wrench on the floor or something, and Dad would have to fix whatever it was himself. Charlie didn't think Tom would help him cook up a plan to make their parents change their minds.

His dad would have made the best Captain Picard. Charlie could tell that by the way he led Charlie's Boy Scout troop and coached his soccer team. You always knew where you stood with him, and he never let you down.

Until now.

"Hi, Dad."

His dad's mostly bald head came up from the dark engine like a moon. He looked surprised, as if he'd forgotten who Charlie was. Like he was already practicing to be a weekend dad. "Oh! Hi, son. I thought you were Tom for a minute." He leaned back into the engine.

"Dad?"

"Yes, Charlie?" His dad's voice sounded hollow, down there in the engine, and Charlie didn't know what to say. He was going to say something that would make his father think about what he and his mother were going to do. But he didn't know what that was. How could anything be big enough, smart enough, to change grownup minds that were already made up?

"Just tell me if you need anything," Charlie said. "I'll get it for you."

"Thanks, son," his father said. "I'm about through here." Charlie waited. He took his soccer ball from the plastic trash can that was full of balls of every kind, and kicked it around a little. At last his father came up out of the engine wiping his hands on a greasy rag. His father smiled but his eyes looked sad and tired. "You had a pretty good season this year, son," he said. "I think soccer just might be your game. What do you think?"

Charlie hugged the ball against his chest and looked up at his father, brimful of mixed-up feelings he didn't know how to sort out. How could you be mad at a father who kept on plugging for you even though you were the team's absolute klutziest player?

How could you not be mad at a father who was getting ready to leave you?

"You gonna be coach next year?"

"Well, sure," his father said, frowning. "Why wouldn't I be?"

Charlie shrugged. "I dunno. I just figured . . ." He shrugged again, looking at the old house with its screened-in porch looming grayish-white in the dark, instead of at his father.

"Hey." His father laid both his hands on Charlie's shoulders. "Look at me, Charlie."

Charlie did as he was told.

"I said nothing was going to change, didn't I? Your mother and I don't want—"

"That's not true!" Charlie twisted away from his father, feeling hot tears crowd his throat. "Will you be here for dinner? Every night? Just like now?"

"Well, no, but—"

"So how can you say nothing's gonna change? How about *Robinson Crusoe*? Are you still gonna read to me at night? Are we even gonna finish *Robinson Crusoe*? Are we?"

"Of course we will. We'll read when you stay at the condo. What's come over you, Charlie? I thought you, of all the kids—" He sighed. He put his hand lightly on Charlie's back and led him toward the house. "Things will change a little. They have to. Maybe it will seem like a lot to you. To you kids. But your mother and I—"

Charlie spun around so that he was looking straight in his father's eyes. His words came out like spit.

"You're getting a divorce, aren't you? Why don't you just tell the truth!" He was crying now, coughing like a big fat baby, but he couldn't help it. He wanted to hurl himself at his father and beat him with his fists. Instead, he turned and ran for the house, slamming the screen door behind him.

3

Charlie's room was minuscule (another word from his final list), but it was the best one in the house. It was all the way at the top, just under the roof. His ceiling came down on both sides like a tent. From a tiny push-out window he looked out across the valley, where lights were scattered like Wesley's fireflies. He would stare out his tiny window and listen to the room talk, the roof cooling from the day's heat, the hundred-year-old floorboards creaking. The house had been his grandparents' and, before that, his great-grandparents'. He didn't think the walls had heard the D word in all that time.

So many things had changed in Oakhurst since his grandparents' day. His grandpa had been a cattle-man and so had the Bascombs before him, all the way back to the pioneers. Sometimes Charlie thought about those pioneers who came all the way to California but stopped before they got to the ocean. He tried to see the land he lived on as they saw it, rich prairie land that went on forever, then gently climbed into the foothills of blue-gray mountains. You could still see those mountains, but the land between had houses now, even a subdivision. His family had held out the longest before selling—first the cattle, then the land. Twenty acres was all they had left, a "postage stamp," his dad said. Then his dad went back to college and got his teaching credentials. Now he taught English at the local high school. He never really liked cows a whole lot, and neither did Charlie's mother. Her life didn't change much, though. She still grew the best vegetables in the country on the land they had left, and sold them on Saturdays at the farmers' market.

Had selling the land made it easier to give up on other things?

Charlie plunked himself on his bed and stared up at the ceiling, where he'd stuck a bunch of funky plastic glow-in-the-dark stars. He knew his mother would be coming up to check on him. It was her job to soothe hurt feelings, though it was usually Tom's or Carrie's feelings that needed soothing. Charlie felt—he searched his vocabulary for the right word—*righteous*. He felt a little like a jerk for losing his temper and for crying like a wienie, but he also felt righteous. His parents were wrong. His father especially. He didn't know why his father more than his mother, but that was how he felt. Righteous and angry and resolute. He was going to fix this mess. Somehow. And words weren't going to do it. He knew that now. He had to *do* something. Something to make them see . . .

And then it came to him, as if the walls had whispered in his ear. There *was* something he could do. It was scary, almost too scary to try. But this was important. If it worked, and it had to, he could save his family.

"Charlie? You up here?" His mother appeared at the top of the steps. His dinosaur night-light covered her face and arms with strange green skin. Her hair looked like green spaghetti. He didn't answer at first. He wanted her to worry. "Charlie? Honey?" She came over and sat on the edge of his bed. "You okay, sweetie?"

"I'm okay," he mumbled.

"Why don't you come down and have some cake and ice cream? Just you and me. We'll eat the whole cake and nobody else will have any. How's that?"

Little Mister Sunshine would have laughed at her joke. He'd have hopped right up and followed his mom down the stairs. He'd have eaten two pieces of cake and two bowls of ice cream just to please her. But doing what his mother wanted him to do wasn't going to make his parents change their minds. "Nah," he said. "I mean, no thanks."

"Are you sure you're okay, Charlie?" She reached her hand out to brush back the hair that hung in his face. "Dad said—"

He scooched away from her, toward the sloping

wall, so that she couldn't reach him. "I'm okay." There was a cold hard knot in his stomach that kept him from crying.

"That's my boy," she said. "I told Daddy you'd be all right. Sometimes it seems like, I don't know, like you're my *oldest* child. You seem to understand so much for an eleven-year-old." She was quiet for a few minutes. Then she blew her nose and he knew she was crying again. "Your father and I have tried so hard to make things work . . ."

He heard her sigh in the dark. She patted his thigh and he felt the bedsprings release as she stood. "You know how sorry we are, don't you, honey?" This time she waited.

"Yes, I know."

He felt her warmth as she leaned over and planted a kiss on his forehead. "I know the minute I leave you're going to turn on your light and read until midnight, aren't you?"

"Nuh-uh." He was only half listening because now he knew what he had to do to make his parents change their minds.

She laughed. "Sure you are. Well, it's summer, you don't have to get up for school. Did you brush your teeth?"

"No."

It had to be something Charlie Bascomb would never do.

"Well, don't you forget."

"I won't."

Something that Little Mister Sunshine would never do in a million years.

"Charlie?"

"Yes?" He wouldn't go too far. He didn't want to turn up on the side of a milk carton or anything. He just needed to teach his parents a lesson, make them realize what a broken family felt like before it was too late. He *had* to and this was the only way he could think of.

"You sure you're all right?"

"Uh-huh." And he was. Because he knew, sure as he'd known every last word on the sixth-grade final vocabulary list, that he'd come up with the very thing that would make his parents change their minds.

He couldn't lose. Like his dad said, there wasn't a darned thing you couldn't get done if you just put your mind to it.

4

Charlie lay listening to the house creak and groan as it settled from the heat of the day into the coolness of night. Earlier, he'd heard the screen door screech and bang several times but didn't know whether or not everybody was home now. He guessed that his father had probably come inside because the lights went out in the garage, but Tom could still be out there, somewhere in the night. He could be *getting into trouble.*

Those were the words his parents had begun to use lately when they argued about Tom. Getting into trouble meant running around with the wrong kids, the ones from the city, the ones who dyed their hair green or orange and wore rings in places besides their fingers and ears. Kids who smoked cigarettes or worse things. Charlie hoped that Tom had come home. That everybody was in their beds.

He read until it was really late, but it was hard to

concentrate, even though *Swiss Family Robinson* was one of his favorite books. It used to remind him of his family, some of the adventures they'd have when they took a car trip out into the country, or the one really great time when they went backpacking in Yosemite. But that was *before*. When they were a perfect family.

When he realized his eyes were closed, Charlie pulled back from the warm beckoning cave of sleep and sat up. He looked at the floor, his first problem. It moaned and groaned something terrible—everything talked in this house—but he knew the worst places and avoided those as he made his way to his closet. Inside, he moved things around very quietly until he uncovered his camping equipment. When he'd gotten his sleeping bag, cooking gear, stove, and ground cloth stuffed inside his backpack, he began to fill the pockets with other things he thought he might need—his pocketknife, first-aid kit, matches, compass, and flashlight. He opened his top drawer and looked for a minute at the sash on which he'd begun to collect his merit badges. Boy Scouts were geeks, Carrie had informed him, everybody said so. But Charlie was proud of his badges and would keep the sash forever. There were badges for the easy things, like camping and cooking, but harder ones, too, like sailing and CPR. He hoped he never had to sail a boat by himself or resuscitate somebody who was having a heart attack, but at least he knew how.

Money. He knew exactly how much he had, $43.75,

and didn't think he would need all of it. Still, he wrapped the bills around the coins and tucked the small package into the pocket of his jeans, which were lying on the chair where he'd tossed them. He got dressed. From the squeaky bureau drawer, pulled quietly toward his chest, he took a clean T-shirt, underwear, and socks. Then, because he looked far too much like his normal self, he put on an old red cowboy hat that had been hanging on a nail over his bed so long he'd stopped seeing it. The hat had been too big for a six-year-old but it fit just fine now. He pulled it low over his eyes and decided that was the way he would wear it.

It was a struggle getting into the heavy backpack without someone to hold it from behind, but he managed, balancing the frame on his bed and then sliding into the straps. A feeling of purpose settled into his shoulders with the backpack. He was really going to do this thing. He *was*. And life would change back to the way it had been before. Before the big announcement dinner. Before his parents had lost their minds.

He realized after a few minutes that he was just standing in the middle of the floor, all suited up. Was he nuts? What did he think he was doing? His parents would go crazy. His mother could, like, flip out or something. Really flip out and have to be put in some mental hospital. Could that happen? He didn't really think so but, still, he should leave some sort of note, at least do that. So they didn't think some madman had climbed up the drainpipe and snatched him from his bed.

"Dear Mom and Dad," he wrote at the top of a piece of lined school paper. "I am going away. It is just too sad to stay here right now with the way things are. Don't concern yourself about me too much. I will be fine. Perchance you will change your minds and I can come back home to live with you again. Your son, Charlie."

He looked at his blocky writing and thought that what he'd said was just right. Mr. Whitcomb, his sixth-grade teacher, would have been proud that Charlie included two of the year's vocabulary words, *concern* and *perchance*. He especially liked *perchance*. It made him sound grownup and serious.

He read the note again. It was so sad he felt like crying himself.

5

It took forever to get all the way down the stairs, holding his breath, stepping around the noisy spots, tiptoeing past the den, where his dad was sleeping now. In the kitchen he eased a cupboard open, took the last two granola bars, a can of tuna, and a package of hot-chocolate mix. He crossed the checkered floor of the moonlit kitchen on his way to the front door, the back one being too near the garage, where the dogs would hear him and send up an alarm. Against the far wall was a huge square shadow of himself and he walked into it, his shadow and himself becoming one at the door to the dark hallway.

The house felt strange in the middle of the night. More alive somehow, alert and breathing calmly, as if it were guarding his family as they slept.

Outside on the wide front porch he took a deep breath of the night air. It still had a tinge of warmth left over from the blistering heat of the August afternoon. Charlie looked up at a full white moon and told himself that he wasn't afraid. That there was nothing to be afraid of.

As he crossed the yard to the dirt road, a wood dove called to its mate, a low trill Charlie had heard dozens of times in the night. Glancing back over his shoulder to make sure no one had heard him leave, he saw that the windows were all dark. He settled his pack on his shoulders, hung his thumbs from the straps, and headed for the main road.

What was he forgetting? Something didn't seem right. But not until he got to the main road did he realize what it was. The wood dove's mate hadn't returned its call. Or, if it had, Charlie, sunk deep in his thoughts, hadn't heard.

There was little traffic on the paved road at any time of day and none this time of night. The Bascomb house was officially in the country but, as his father often said with a sad shake of his head, the country was disappearing as fast as his hair. At Four Corners, where the narrow paved road met the highway, there was a brand-new gas station on one corner and an all-night doughnut shop on another. A sign on the third corner announced that a Major Supermarket would soon be on that spot, and then, as his father said, it was all downhill from there. His parents vowed that they would never sell the old house or any of the remaining land, but his father was the one who loved the country best and he was moving into a condo. His mother was thrilled about the new supermarket. She told him so, then swore him to secrecy.

Maybe he should stay and make sure they didn't sell the house, too. But he couldn't do *everything*.

He pulled his shoulder straps and settled the pack more firmly on his shoulders. With the moon behind him, his shadow stretched out ten feet ahead and lent him courage.

A quarter mile down the road he came to the Carters'. All the Carter kids were grown and gone and Charlie had never met them. In the front yard, mostly dirt, were two broken-down cars and an old washing machine. Someone had coated a tire with white paint and planted a geranium inside. For a while, bright red flowers stuck up from the center of the tire, but they dried up and died. Waiting at the school-bus stop in front of the Carter house, the kids Charlie knew had plenty to say about the Carters. Old man Carter beat his dogs good, they said. That's why there was a chain lying in the yard but no dogs. They'd all run off. The kids whispered about worse things, too. Things that were done to the children when they were young. Things Charlie didn't like to think about and didn't want to believe.

He liked the sound his hiking boots made in the soft dirt on the side of the road, a solid *wump, wump*. His dad had bought everyone top-quality hiking boots for the Yosemite trip, all except Wesley, who wasn't born yet. His mother had put up a fuss over the expense but his dad insisted. On the trail that summer he would often stop and ask them if they weren't glad they had those great hiking boots, and they would all, together, with serious faces, tell him that yes, they were sooooo glad. After a while it became a family joke. They would see who could hold out the longest without cracking up when his father would stop in the middle of the trail, for no reason at all, and turn and ask them if they weren't real glad . . .

Charlie had loved the backpacking vacation more than anyone because he'd gotten to practice what he'd learned as a Cub Scout. He became the fire builder, the site chooser, the map reader, and for a while it seemed that everyone was relying on him for everything. Were there bears nearby? Was the water safe to drink? Could you eat these little green things?

Then, for the first time, wumping along the side of the road, head-high weeds in ragged shadow beside him, Charlie wondered if his family might have been having a joke on him. That his father wasn't the only one they were laughing at. But they'd all had a great time. Even Carrie, who had begged and pleaded to stay behind with friends.

On the last night of the vacation his dad had made this corny fireside speech about family, about the *strength of family bonds*—his exact words. Charlie could still see his father's face, the way his eyes welled up, so that he had to look down. Charlie thought he'd die of embarrassment, and of love, and of all the other deeper things he had no words for.

Now he thought: What about *that*, Dad? He saw himself saying, in his *face*, in the face of his six-foot father: What about the *strength of family bonds?*

A rustle in the field made him jump and he reached around into a zippered pocket of his backpack and took out his pocketknife. Farther down the road, knowing the rustle for the rat it probably was, he put the knife back in his pack. But his heart knocked for a long time and his stomach had the hollow feeling he recognized as fear.

He'd been walking for hours, it seemed, and hadn't yet gotten to the highway. Always before, he'd been in the car with one of his parents and the distance seemed like nothing. If he turned around now, he thought he could get back before anybody woke up, even his father, who got up with the sun. But if he didn't make it all the way back to the house before first light, he'd feel like a jerk. He'd have gone through all this for nothing.

So he began to sing. Campfire songs, army songs, trail songs he'd learned in Boy Scouts, first softly to himself, then—because no one but snakes and rats and night birds would hear him anyway—he sang at the top of his lungs. That carried him to the end of the field, but his legs were tired and his stomach felt empty. He felt like a mule, all weighted down and weary.

So he made himself think about cream-filled choco-late-covered doughnuts, his favorite. He thought how good they were to bite into, first the chocolate frosting, then the pudding-like cream. He thought what a mess they made of your chin and your fingers, and that the mess helped to make them as good as they were.

There were a few more houses on this stretch but they were far back from the road and settled, as his own, in sleep. A dog barked from behind one of the houses but no lights came on and Charlie trudged on, unseen. When a car appeared in the distance, only pinpoints of light at first, he hunkered down behind a tree and waited, his heart bursting, until an old junker passed, spewing exhaust fumes and loud music in its wake. Somebody Tom knew, Charlie guessed. Then: *Tom!* It could have been Tom in that car. Tom might have caught him. The thought made his stomach weak and he didn't move from his spot behind the tree until the sound of the old car was blotted up by the night.

He thought, once, about making camp in the last thin patch of woods before the main highway but he knew he had to do his traveling in the dark or be caught and sent home, so he trudged on toward Four Corners, songless, his head and feet aching.

6

Four Corners Donut sat on the corner of Wright Road and Highway 41 like a stranded lighthouse, so bright it made your eyeballs ache. Charlie pushed open the door to the smell of cold grease. Behind the counter a minuscule man in a bright white uniform was reading a newspaper. Charlie waited. At last the man looked up like a sleepy turtle and blinked.

"One chocolate-covered cream, please," Charlie said. He saw that the newspaper was written in one of those languages that ran curling down the page. "And some milk."

The man peered at Charlie out of his bird-bright yellow-brown eyes for a long time before turning away. Charlie waited for the man to get his doughnut from the case where four doughnuts and a dried-out cinnamon bun lay on greasy white paper. He saw it as an omen, a lucky sign, that one of the doughnuts was his favorite chocolate-covered cream. The old man took Charlie's money into his crinkled dark palm, frowned at it, and put it in the register. "You out late," the man said. "Boy like you."

Charlie didn't know what to say without lying, so he just took the doughnut and milk to a booth and sat down. He listened to the buzz of the fluorescent lights and the pages of the newspaper turning while he wolfed down his doughnut. Already it felt as if he'd been gone an awfully long time, and he thought it was funny, funny-strange, that his parents were still sleeping and didn't even know yet that he was gone.

Charlie was licking chocolate off his fingers when he heard the door open. In came a girl wearing a short watermelon-green skirt and shiny black knee-high boots. She stomped up to the counter and ordered a cup of black coffee. Her leather jacket, the kind motorcycle guys wore, was about twenty sizes too big. For a second or two the old man didn't do anything, just stared at the girl, who was taller than he was and real skinny. Her skin was so pale she almost blended into the light. The man finally turned away, and the girl clicked her long purple fingernails on the counter.

"One-oh-seven," the man said, pushing a take-out cup, steam rising, toward the girl.

"A buck seven? You gotta be kidding. Out here in hickville? A buck seven for a cup of coffee? No way!"

The old man waited, his face unchanged.

The girl poked through some coins in her hand.

"Cripes," she said, disgusted, and then, as if she knew all along that Charlie had been watching, said: "Hey, cowboy, you got a quarter?"

Charlie felt his jaw drop open and then he felt stupid because he was supposed to say something back. Yes or no. So he said yes and dug a quarter out of his pocket.

"Cool," the girl said. She clomped over to Charlie, snatched the quarter, and clomped back to the counter, where she dumped her small pile of change. Blowing on her coffee, she came back to Charlie's booth. "What's your name?"

Charlie's name popped right out of his mouth before his mind had the chance to say that maybe he shouldn't tell the truth. After all, he was a *fugitive*. What if she, or the man behind the counter, decided to turn him in?

"Mine's Doo," she said, sliding into the seat across from him. She had narrow green eyes and a tiny gold ring sticking out from her right eyebrow. Her hair was yellow cornsilk. Charlie didn't think she was pretty, exactly, but she was trying hard to be. Or trying hard to be something else, something that wasn't herself. Strings of yellow hair hung in her face and down the back of the big leather jacket. She had rings on every one of her fingers, even her thumbs, and five holes in each of her ears into which all kinds of colored stones and one tiny angel had been poked. Charlie guessed she was about sixteen, Tom's age, and felt kind of proud that she would bother to talk to a kid like him.

Charlie pushed his glasses up his nose. "Do? That's your name?"

"Yeah, weird, huh? My daddy named me that. It's for Doolittle." She spelled it out for Charlie. "It's not my real name, though?"

"Oh."

"Only my best friends know what that is, my real name."

"Oh," said Charlie again, and thought he ought to do better. Ought to say something back, but he couldn't think of a thing to say. He thought the old man was watching them, but when he looked up, he saw that he was reading his strange newspaper.

"Where you off to?" asked Doo. Her chin jerked toward his backpack that he'd set in the seat beside him.

Charlie shrugged. "Nowhere," he said.

"You're running away, aren't you?" Charlie's heart went up behind his teeth, but then she said: "Don't worry, I'm not gonna tell nobody. Why you runnin'?" He could tell by some of her words, the way she cut them off, that she was from somewhere else, maybe from the South. His Aunt Charlotte was from Alabama and this girl sounded a little like her.

"No reason," he said, looking down at hands that were small and sunbrowned. He hadn't washed them before bed and there were ridges of dirt in the creases. "Just because."

"Your dad beat you?" She leaned toward him, as if

she wanted to pull out all his secrets. He could smell her chewing gum and a trace of something else. Cigarettes. When he shook his head, she said: "Worse, huh? Bummer."

Charlie didn't know what to say. He felt like he should defend his father, who'd never hit him harder than a swipe with a dishtowel, but he couldn't exactly tell her that he was running away to keep his family together. She probably wouldn't understand. She might even try to talk him out of it.

"My old man's so cool," she said. Her chewing gum cracked loudly several times. "I'm going to visit him. Well, probably stay with him?" A lot of what she said turned up at the end, like a question, even when it wasn't one. "Can't go back home, that's for sure."

"Oh," said Charlie, having lost whatever words he ever knew.

"That's okay, you can ask. I ain't got *no* secrets!" She laughed and slouched back against the seat. "My stepfather? You name it, he did it. A real creep! If my real dad knew, he'd kill him!"

"Are you going to tell?"

"Maybe," she said. "Depends. Besides, I fixed things myself before I left." Her laugh had a bitter edge. "Fixed them good." He watched her wet the tip of her finger and stick it into his doughnut crumbs, then lick her finger clean.

"What did you do?"

She fixed her green eyes on his face and he could see that she was about to tell him what she'd done, but something made her change the subject. "My dad lives in L.A. Figure I'll get there by tomorrow." She slumped back in the seat and took a crumpled package of cigarettes out of her pocket. "I'd offer you one, but you don't look like you ought to be smoking, if you excuse my saying so. Like, you're how old? Twelve, thirteen?"

"Yeah," said Charlie, crossing his fingers under the table. "Thirteen. Almost."

"Well, hey, I can give you a ride. Depending on where you're going. Guy like you shouldn't be traveling alone. All kinds of creeps out there."

"Oh, that's okay," Charlie said. He didn't want to hurt the girl's feelings but she *was* a stranger, after all, and there were rules about that. And, besides, he wasn't going all that far. Just far enough to make a point. As soon as his parents changed their minds, he'd head for home.

The old man had somehow gotten himself to the side of their table without making a sound. Charlie and Doo looked up at the same time, and there he was.

"How old you?" he demanded, peering down at Charlie out of his yellow-brown eyes.

"What's it to you?" said Doo with a jerk of her pointy chin. "You don't have to tell him, Charlie. It's not, like, a law or anything." So Charlie said nothing, though his insides cringed at the girl's bad manners.

"You go home now," said the old man. "Too late for you. No good this girl!" He shooed his hand at Doo as if to brush her away like a pesky fly.

"Butt out," said Doo.

"I call police," the man said and turned toward a pay phone that hung on the back wall.

"Come on," said Doo to Charlie, sliding out of the booth. "He means it."

Charlie froze. His mind played a quick game of Ping-Pong: Doo or the police. He grabbed his pack and ran behind Doo out the door.

"This way," Doo yelled over her shoulder, her hair flinging into her face. He followed her around the back of a Dumpster. "Ta-dah!" she said proudly and there was a bright yellow Volkswagen. You could see its chrome engine, the whole thing, because there was no back lid. Out of the engine stuck two shiny chrome pipes, like antennae. Doo popped the hood and Charlie threw in his pack.

7

They squealed onto the highway, the little Bug's engine so loud Charlie could barely hear the good-boy voice in his head saying that he had done a terrible thing: he had gotten into a car with a stranger. The wind nearly took his hat, but when he tried to roll the window up, there wasn't any, so he just closed his eyes, put his head back, and tried to think about what would happen next. What he would do next.

"You can crawl into the back if you need to crash," said Doo. Then she flipped on the tiny radio. Rock music thundered against four sides of Charlie's head and beat against his rib cage. Doo yelled: "Quads!" Meaning the speakers, and Charlie nodded, trying to look just the right amount of impressed. Doo's chin went up and down. She beat her fingers against the steering wheel. The familiar landscape zipped past his open window: The Roundup, where they bought Molly's oats; the chicken farm where his mother sent Tom on Sundays to get a fresh chicken. Were there stale chickens? Charlie was beginning to get nervous. The world was zipping by too fast: the blue-painted water tower, the long patch of dark woods—shorter than he ever thought—John Muir Elementary. He saw the windows of his sixth-grade classroom and then they were gone. Gray clouds floated like pond scum across the moon. Doo cracked her gum so loud he could hear it over the music. The engine wound to such a pitch that Charlie thought it might blow up. His head began to ache.

They drove until Charlie didn't know the scenery anymore. He guessed they were in Pinedale, and after that he just lost track. He tried not to think about his family, about how far behind he was leaving them, but he couldn't help it. Things they did together, things he'd forgotten all about, kept flashing in his mind as if he were drowning.

At last Doo pulled the car over to the side of the road. "Can't keep my eyes open no more," she said, cutting the engine. She got out of the car and stretched her long arms at the sky, which was dotted with a world of stars and planets a billion miles away. Charlie had never felt so alone in all his life. The sudden silence was creepy. "You go ahead and catch a ride with somebody else if you want. I gotta get some sleep." Then she climbed like a long-legged spider into the backseat.

Charlie got out of the car. He stared ahead at the

empty road swallowed up by a dark mouth at the far end, then at the deep silent woods that ran alongside. He choked down his heart, which had settled in his throat. He gave an exaggerated carefree shrug and said in an almost steady voice: "I'll just go ahead and set up camp here."

Blueberry, swoon, scalawag, sylvan . . .

Doo yawned. "Whatever," she said.

Charlie popped the hood of the little yellow car and took out his gear. He fished in the side pocket of his pack for his flashlight and, when he found it, shined it into the woods. He tried to tell himself that it was just like the time he and his family camped in Yosemite, but it wasn't. Still, he knew what he had to do.

He lugged his pack to a clearing just a little way into the trees. If he wasn't that far from the car, he told himself, he'd know when Doo was ready to go in the morning. He'd hear the car start up. But the truth was in his shaking fingers as he set his pack against a rock and began to make camp: he was afraid.

The woods were very quiet. Too quiet. He could hear nothing but the sound of his own rustling and his breathing as he laid out his ground cloth and unrolled his sleeping bag. Shining his flashlight all around, he wondered if he should make a small fire. Then whatever made their home in these woods would leave him alone. There were bears, he knew that, though nobody had seen one for a very long time.

And coyotes and bobcats.

Snakes.

He slid quickly into his bag and zipped it up to his chin. Then, when he was perfectly quiet, all the things that had held their breath while he made his camp came skittering to life. Charlie drew up his knees. He pulled the bag up around his ears. He began to count backwards from a hundred, but the noise lifted all around him like a symphony. A bug symphony.

When he was small and something frightened him in the middle of the night, an unfamiliar sound, a bad dream, he knew just where to go. Straight into his parents' bedroom, where he would snuggle against one or the other while he drifted down into the well of safety that was sleep. Now only his mother slept in the big four-poster bed. His father watched TV late into the night and slept on the "dog couch." Charlie found him there a bunch of times, the first time because Oakie was whining outside and nobody heard her but him. After that, he was curious. Something wasn't right. School had just ended and they hadn't planned a vacation. Something wasn't right. He went to Tom.

"Dad's got a girlfriend," Tom said. But Charlie didn't think that could be true. He still didn't. He tried picturing his father holding some lady's hand. Kissing some redheaded lady who looked like Bonnie Raitt, his father's favorite singer. His father was too old for girlfriends. It was dumb. He was still pretty sure Tom made it up.

But, if he didn't have a girlfriend, why was he moving into a condo? He *hated* condos.

Charlie let go of his fistful of worries as sleep came on.

And suddenly he was awake. Awake and aware of exactly where he was. Something had moved. More than one something, just behind his head. He held his breath and listened harder. There it was again, a shuffle, then another. Some breathing. His knife! Why wasn't it in his pocket? He had forgotten the first rule: Be Prepared. And now he was at the mercy of whatever was standing in back of his head. He reached his hand inch by inch toward his flashlight and pulled it inside his bag. More rustling. His heartbeat and the rustling, no other sound.

He could yell for Doo. But what good would she be against . . . *them*!

He did the only thing he could think to do. He rolled and half stood, his sleeping bag over his head, and bellowed in the loudest, deepest voice he had. He aimed his light where the sound had come from.

They stared back, three fully grown raccoons, their ringed eyes amused.

"Shoo!" Charlie yelled. But they stood their ground, not the least frightened of him. As he watched they ambled over to his pack and began sorting through it. Out came Charlie's down vest and his cooking gear. The largest of the animals stepped on his cowboy hat and crushed it. Charlie picked up a stick and beat the ground. He didn't want to get closer than necessary to the animals, who seemed each about half his size.

His food bag dangled from a branch a good distance off the ground, but he knew raccoons were smart enough to get it down if they spotted it, so he kept yelling and beating the ground to distract them. At last, bored, they ambled off into the woods.

Charlie lay back down, his heart thudding. Either Doo slept like a hibernating bear or she'd heard the whole commotion and let Charlie fend for himself.

For a long time, he lay on his back counting stars. At last, dizzy with fatigue, he drifted off.

8

When Charlie awoke, Doo was standing over him, staring down, fists on her hipbones. She wore a skinny white undershirt thing with her bra straps showing. Through the shirt Charlie could see the outline of her ribs. Her chest was flat as his own, almost. "I should get me one of those bags," she said. She leaned over and peered into his backpack. "Got anything to eat in here?"

Charlie scrambled out of his bag. "Sure," he said. "Up there." He pointed at the bag dangling from the branch above their heads. When he got it down, Doo went right through it, just like a raccoon.

"Whoa!" she said, pulling out the cocoa mix. "Hot chocolate! Too bad we can't make it."

"We can," said Charlie. He took out his camp stove, unfolded its legs, and set it on the ground. Then he attached the stove to the fuel canister. Doo watched wide-eyed. Her mouth twitched as if it wanted to break into a big fat grin but she wouldn't let it. "How did you learn all this stuff, anyway?"

"Boy Scouts mostly," he admitted. There were bigger things to worry about than being a geek.

"You're kidding! I didn't think they had Boy Scouts anymore."

"Sure they do." He nodded toward his pack. "There's some cooking gear in the bottom of that." While Doo searched for it, Charlie lit a match. The stove started right up with a little pop and Charlie adjusted the flame.

"This it?" Doo handed him his prized set of cooking gear, a tiny pot and plate and cup nested together and secured with a wing nut. Charlie set the pot on the stove and shook the powdered chocolate into it. Then he poured in water from his canteen.

"This is so cool!" Doo said. Her blond hair was all ratted up and there were dark circles under her eyes. "I mean, you got everything you need. Like you could cross the whole country and just be, like, on your own." She held the tiny metal cup in both hands and sipped at the warm chocolate. Her green eyes gazed past Charlie, off into the woods and beyond, out to a place only she could see.

"Yeah . . ." said Charlie, who'd gone much farther than he'd ever expected to. Already he'd broken one of the Boy Scout laws, *A Scout is trustworthy*, by telling Doo he was thirteen instead of the eleven that he was.

The obedience rule was probably shot, too. Even though his folks never actually *told* him he couldn't run away from home, as a Scout First Class (almost) he knew better.

He handed Doo a granola bar. They munched their breakfast in silence, Doo leaning against a tree with her pale skinny legs sticking straight out, Charlie tending his stove.

Doo smoked a cigarette while Charlie broke camp, gathering up the granola bar wrapper that Doo had dropped on the ground, rolling up his bag, tucking away his cooking gear. He felt grownup and in charge.

Until he thought about his folks.

His father would already have gotten up and put on the coffee pot. His mother would be changing Wesley, maybe singing to him as she always did. Charlie could almost hear her in his mind. She had a soft, raspy voice he loved even more than he loved words. After a while, not yet, they'd start to wonder where he was. His mother would call up the stairs: "Charlie?" When he didn't answer, she'd call again. Then his mother would go up the thirteen steps. She'd probably be lugging Wesley. She'd say something about sleepyheads or slugabeds. She'd try to be her same self, the one she was before. Then she'd see he wasn't in his bed.

And then she'd find his note.

Doo blew three perfect smoke rings. They drifted up into the trees, growing larger and fainter as they rose. "So what's your story, Charlie?" Doo said at last. "I mean"—she twirled her hand around—"you got all this stuff? You got nice clothes? You just having yourself a little adventure or what?"

Charlie frowned and jerked at one of the zippers on his pack, as if it were stuck. When he looked up, he saw that she was going to wait him out. So he told her about his folks, about their big announcement, about his plan to go away until they decided to stay together.

It wouldn't take that long, he said. He began to repack his stuff.

"Whoa!" Doo shook her head several times in disbelief. "Whoa! You really think they're gonna change their lives just like that"—she snapped her fingers—for *you?* Because you *tell* them to. Because you *threaten* them?"

"Well . . ." Charlie blinked several times. He wasn't quite as certain as he was before, but he shrugged as if he were. "Sure," he said.

"Whoa," said Doo. "Never happen." She stubbed her cigarette into the ground.

"*You* don't know,? said Charlie, his plan unraveling before his eyes like the back of the sofa after the cats had gotten to it.

"Look," she said. "You gotta do this thing right. You can't, like, call them on the phone and say, 'Hey, it's Charlie and I'm all right and, by the way, are you still gonna get a divorce?' " She rolled her eyes.

Charlie bit his tongue, thinking that was just about what he had in mind. He picked up his red cowboy hat. It was flat as a Frisbee.

"Nah," said Doo. "You gotta play this thing out. Really give them a good scare. If I was you, I wouldn't call them for a month."

"A month?" The hair on the back of Charlie's neck stood on end.

"Well, a couple of weeks at least. You want them to know you mean business."

Charlie thought with a sinking heart that she was probably right. His parents had to believe he would stay away forever, that he could live on his own without them. That he would really do it unless they stayed together.

"You might as well come with me to L.A.," Doo said. "My dad'll know what to do. Maybe he'll, like, negotiate. You know, with your folks?"

"Oh, yeah . . ." Charlie said, uncertainly.

"Anyway, it's an idea," said Doo, lighting up another cigarette. "It's a serious thing, being out on the road. Sometimes you gotta do it, though. Sometimes you got no choice, right?" She looked at Charlie then, her green eyes sad. "My ma? I try to help her but, like, there's no way. She and Manny? My stepdad? They get going around happy hour—that's what they call it. Happy hour, no lie! So like they're drinking and laughing, sometimes they put on these old records—not CDs or nothing—those old black plastic things? And they dance and they're all lovey-dovey. But they're putting away the booze like nothing you ever seen!"

Charlie wasn't sure he wanted to hear the rest of the

story. He knew it couldn't turn out good. But Doo went on, talking sometimes to her cigarette, sometimes to Charlie, but mostly, it seemed, to herself.

"And then it starts getting ugly. My ma will say something, nothing bad, you know. Just . . . something. Something silly or just normal. But Manny, he starts getting weird. Starts taking everything wrong. At first, he just gives her a little push? On the shoulder or something. 'Manny,' Ma says. 'Don't, honey.' I can hear she's afraid. Already she's afraid because Manny's just winding up. And then he starts in. He's serious now. He's yelling about something really stupid, something that didn't even happen. That happened in his head. He's yelling, calling my ma names like you wouldn't believe. And then he slaps her. A love tap, he calls it. But my ma is cringing against the wall and she's crying 'cause she can see what's coming like a car wreck. And me? I know I'm next . . ."

Doo brushed the tears away from her eyes before they could fall, as if she were angry at them. Angry at the tears, or at herself for crying. She stubbed out her cigarette, brushing the leaves off her bright green skirt. "Let's go, Charlie boy," she said. "We can't hang out in the woods all day."

Right then, to Charlie, that didn't seem like a bad idea. But he picked up the crushed cigarettes, threw his pack over his shoulder, and followed Doo through the trees.

In the car Doo put on her makeup, peering into the

rearview mirror, smearing on lipstick the color of cotton candy. A hay truck flew by and the little Bug rattled, shaking Doo's hand. She swore into the mirror. Charlie made a breathless wish on the load of hay that his father would never leave home, that the girlfriend would disappear, that his family would stay together. That he could trust Doo with his life, at least for now.

Doo started the car and looked over at Charlie, her hand on the shift knob. "Look, people split up all the time. My ma's been married three times. No, four, if you count Manny. It's, like, not the end of the world. You sure you don't wanna go back home?" Charlie shook his head. Doo turned the key and the little Bug coughed. A cloud of gray smoke billowed from the chrome exhaust pipes. Doo frowned. She cranked the key again. This time, the car started. "Okay, then!" she cried. "L.A., here we come!"

He would call his folks from the city. It was true, what Doo said. People split up all the time. But his folks weren't just any people. And they sure weren't Doo's folks. They'd find him gone and they'd do anything, *anything*, to get him back. That much Charlie knew.

9

At a stop sign in Tranquility, which was another one of Charlie's favorite words, Doo announced that they needed a map. "Look in there," she said, pointing to the glove compartment. "See if there's a map."

Charlie pushed the chrome button and the door to the little box flipped open. He expected to find all the papers and junk that were in his dad's glove box; instead, he found a single map of the State of California, neatly folded. It felt like magic. Like opening a magic box and finding just what you wanted.

See if there's a map, she'd said, as if she didn't know what was in her own glove compartment. Well, his dad couldn't guess half the things that were in his either if you asked him. Still, it seemed funny that Doo didn't know what was in hers, when the map was the only thing.

"You can be the navigator," Doo said. But Charlie didn't need her permission for that. Already he'd spread open the map and begun putting his map-reading skills to work. After all, he'd been the family navigator since Cub Scouts, when he was only seven.

"Just the back roads," said Doo. "The blue ones."

"I know which ones are the back roads," said Charlie, insulted. He traced his finger from Mendota, the last road sign he remembered, down through Kerman and Five Points. Then, puzzled, he looked over at Doo, whose corn-silk hair was flying around her head. "How come the back roads? It'll take longer."

"Well, *duh!*" she said.

Fascinated, Charlie watched Doo poke a cigarette between her lips, then light it one-handed. With matches, not a lighter. And in the wind, too. "I just like the back roads, that's all." She glanced over at Charlie and shrugged. "Well," she said then, "truth is, I ain't been drivin' all that long. The freeways scare me, kind of."

"Well, okay, sure," said Charlie, who always liked the back roads best. "We'll just go down through Hanford and Corcoran . . ."

"Just tell me left and right," she said. "You're the navigator."

Now that he had an important job to do, Charlie felt good. He set to work tracing their route and by the time his finger got to Los Angeles he had convinced himself that his wild ride in the little yellow car blaring rock and roll out its missing windows was just another

Boy Scout trip. Doo rocked to the music, her chin bobbing up and down, fingers drumming the wheel. When she wasn't flipping stations, she was unwrapping a stick of gum or lighting up another cigarette. Once, steering with her left hand, she stuck her face up against the rearview mirror to find something that got caught in her eye. The fact that she could do so many other things while still keeping the little car on the road made her a pretty good driver, or so it seemed to him.

Then, in the middle of nowhere, empty fields fading off into flat gray sky, the engine began to sputter. "Uh-oh," said Doo, pumping the gas, but the little car stalled, coasting slowly to a stop.

Charlie looked ahead at the road that seemed to go on forever without a house or even a car in sight. "Are we out of gas?"

"Nuh-uh." Doo cranked the key again, but the engine just coughed once and died. "I filled it up in Oakhurst. You know, across from that doughnut shop? Just before I saw you." She flipped off the radio and they sat in silence, staring out the window. A pair of hawks glided in lazy circles over the field of dried yellow grass. It was so quiet they could hear each other breathe.

Brow furrowed, Doo chewed on the tip of her thumb. "Guess we'll have to hitch a ride," she said.

Charlie's heart flipped over. "We can't do that!"

"Why not?"

He didn't want to say *Because my folks would kill*

me, but that was the truth. "Well," he shrugged, thinking fast. "We can't just leave the car here. Somebody could just, like, pick it up and take it. It's so *little*."

"Well, yeah, I guess, but—"

"And, besides, there's nobody to hitch a ride with."

"Well, what do *you* think we should do, Mr. Boy Scout?"

He had to have an answer. He thought fast. "Well, we should just . . . just make a plan. A contingency plan." He glanced over at Doo, who looked impressed. His mind raced ahead. "We should, um, just wait a while."

Doo rolled her eyes. "Wait? That's your big plan. Wait for what?"

"Well, for the car to rest up."

"Rest up," she said doubtfully.

"Yeah, you know. Like it's probably overheated. We'll count to five hundred and try to start it again."

"And then what?"

"And then, if it doesn't start, well, that's when we use our contingency plan."

"Which is what?" she said, looking at him the way his mother sometimes did, with her mouth pinched and her eyes disbelieving.

"Count," he ordered. "One, two, three . . ."

They counted. At one hundred Doo began slapping the steering wheel in time with the numbers, so Charlie slapped his knees. "One hundred and *one*! One hundred and *two*!" By the time they got to one hundred sixty-seven, they were yelling the numbers to see who could yell the loudest. "Four hundred ninety-*nine*! Five *hundred*!"

They turned and looked at each other. "Okay, start her up," said Charlie.

Doo crossed her fingers and reached for the key. "Say a blessing," she said.

Charlie laughed. "A blessing? For the car? You're kidding, right?"

"No, I'm not kidding. Don't you believe in God?"

"Well, sure, but—"

"Then say a blessing!" She scowled at Charlie as if all this was his fault somehow. "Okay, then don't." She turned the key, but nothing happened. "See? We shoulda prayed. Or *something*!" She sighed dramatically, like Carrie when things went wrong, as if it was the end of the world. "What now?"

10

An old farm truck came rattling up beside them. It looked just like the one Charlie's father had gotten rid of when they sold off the land. A woman with frizzled gray hair leaned across the seat and bellowed, "Need a hand?"

In the back of the truck were two goats, a large white one and a smaller one that was fawn-colored. They pulled at the rope looped around their necks and their yellow eyes flicked nervously. Doo stared at the goats as if she couldn't figure out what they were. Charlie said, "The car won't start. Could you call somebody for us?"

"I can do better than that," the old woman said. "Hang on." She pulled ahead of the Bug and slowly backed up. When she got out of the truck, she was carrying a coil of rope like the one that kept the goats in the truck. "We'll just pull this little yeller thing. What's it, anyway, one of them German cars? You can never trust no foreign vehicle. ("Ve-hicle," she said, as if it were two words.) "Told my youngest, Denver, don't you go getting you no foreign car when right here in America, the land of Henry Ford, we got us the best cars in the whole entire world, bar none . . ."

She talked nonstop as she tied the rope around each bumper, making knots Charlie knew how to do but probably couldn't do in a rope that thick. She left no slack. That way, she said, Doo wouldn't have to steer the broken-down car and they could all ride together. She looked like a grandma, at least the way a grandma was supposed to look, a country grandma anyway, with her gray hair locked into a bun and a faded yellow housedress and raggedy green sweater with holes in the elbows. But her arms were like men's arms and she wore thick black work boots that looked like men's boots.

"Hop in," she said. "In the front. You don't want them goats chewin' on ye. Mean things."

"Whoa," said Doo, steering a wide berth around the goats and hopping up into the truck.

Charlie hesitated at the door, one foot on the running board, the other on the road. "I'm not supposed to ride with strangers," he said, looking down, embarrassed.

"*Charlie!*" said Doo impatiently.

"It's okay, son." said the woman. "This is what you call a gen-you-wine emergency. My kids, they had the same rule when they was young. More harm probably come to ye out here with the turkey vultures than in this here old truck with a bunch of goats goin' to market." She laughed. "Come on, son," she said. "It's all right."

"He's only thirteen," Doo said, making an excuse for Charlie's strange behavior. Charlie gave her a dirty look and got in.

The woman drove slowly, keeping one eye on the Bug, which followed like a well-trained horse.

By the time they pulled onto an unmarked rutted dirt road, Doo and Charlie knew the names, ages, and occupations of the woman's five children, the birth weights of her six grandchildren, and all the operations that her husband, Xavier, had before he died three years ago.

On the road they passed two junked cars, weeds grown up all around them. One was a dark green Volvo station wagon that made Charlie's heart skip because it looked so much like his dad's. If his dad could see him now, what would he say? Charlie figured he knew, and didn't much want to think about it.

Rounding a bend and splashing through a shallow stream, they came at last to a collection of shacks. One had a porch tacked to the front. On the porch was a car seat where a fat white cat slept in a square of sunlight. All around were bright yellow sour-grass flowers, the kind his mother called weeds, even though they were pretty as the flowers in her garden. A mountain of car parts and tires had grown up beside one of the shacks, and broken-down cars were parked everywhere.

"John!" the woman yelled. "John Turner!"

A head poked over the back side of the car-parts mountain and disappeared again.

"He's coming," she said, and around the mountain came a big man wearing a plaid shirt and greasy blue-jeans.

John Turner's beard was rusty-colored with gray stripes and it covered up most of his face, except for his eyes, which were crinkled and friendly. "Well, Norma, where you been keeping yourself?"

They chatted while the goats in the back danced around, their hooves clicking on the metal floor. Doo, losing patience, poked Charlie in the side. Charlie poked her back. Finally, John Turner said he'd have a look at "the little toy." They all got out of the truck and followed John Turner to the back of the Bug. They watched him wiggle wires and pull out a spark plug. "This here your car?" he asked Doo, after sizing up Charlie first and deciding he was too young to drive.

"Uh . . . yeah," said Doo. "But, like, I don't know much about it."

John Turner muttered something under his breath and shook his head. He tried the ignition, then went back to the engine. He wore his greasy jeans so low beneath his big belly that they were frayed on the bottom from dragging on the ground. "What'cha two doin' out here in Grangeville anyway? Don't see many fancy little cars like this in the country. Do we, Norma?"

The old woman, Norma, and John Turner looked at each other the way adults do when they don't need words.

"Uh, we kind of got lost?" said Doo quickly. "My brother, Charlie, is, like a Boy Scout and all? And he wanted to, you know, be in the trees and all?" She looked nervously at Charlie. "Right, Charlie?"

Charlie swallowed. "Yeah. I like . . . trees." He shrugged and looked at the ground, feeling his nose itch as if it were growing as fast as Pinocchio's. He *did* like trees, but he wasn't Doo's brother. Why did she say that?

"Well," said John Turner, scratching the back of his head, where the hair grew long and curly. "You'all better get back on the highway when we're finished up. Never know what kind of characters you could run into out here."

Norma laughed, slapping a work-hardened hand against John Turner's back. "We're the characters, John. There's good people out here in the country, you know that. There's good people everywhere."

John Turner began pulling things out of the car-part mountain and tossing them aside. "I know there's a generator for one of these little things in this here pile, that's what I know . . ."

"Salt of the earth," she said, smiling fondly at John Turner, who hadn't smiled at anything, even though he seemed to want to.

He searched in the pile until he finally found what he was looking for. He held up the greasy part and frowned at it, as if waiting for it to say something. Then he nodded once and carried it over to the car.

In no time at all, he had the Bug running. "Where did you say you was goin'?" he said.

"L.A.," said Doo.

"Los Angeles," said Charlie at the same time.

"Our grandpa's dying," said Doo, her eyes wide and sad. "We gotta get there quick!"

"Oh, poor dears," said Norma. Her big hand went to her heart. "I was going to take you to my place for a nice warm meal, you both being so skinny and all. But if you gotta get to your grandpappy, well, you'd better get on the road. The Lord bless you. And your little yeller car, too."

Doo smirked at Charlie, as if to say, "See?"

Above his thick beard, John Turner's eyes studied Doo and Charlie. "Your folks let you drive all that way?"

"Oh, we had to," said Doo quickly. " 'Cause we don't have any folks. I mean, they died in a car crash last year. Drunk driver. So we, like, we live with our aunt." She bit her lip. "And she doesn't drive."

"You poor lambs," said Norma, tears welling up in

her eyes, but John Turner just frowned and squinted at Doo, his arms crossed over his big belly.

Charlie took his savings out of his pocket. "We probably don't have enough money to pay you," he said to John Turner, "but we can send you the rest."

"No charge," said John Turner, his hands tucked into his armpits.

"But—"

"Oh, he won't take a thing," said Norma. "Believe me, I know. You ain't the first to break down out here."

"Well, hey, thanks!" said Doo and hopped right into the driver's seat.

Charlie clutched the door handle on the passenger side. He knew Doo and he shouldn't just hop in the car and drive off with hardly a thank you when these people had been so good to them. "We could do some chores or something," he said doubtfully, staring up at the car-part mountain.

For the first time, John Turner smiled. He had a toothless jack-o-lantern smile. "No need, son. You'll be doin' us both a favor if you keep yourself safe. Hear?"

Charlie nodded. "Thank you, sir," he said. "And thank you, too, Mrs. . . . Norma."

As they zipped down the dirt road, Charlie watched John Turner and Norma growing smaller in the side-view mirror. They were waving, just like grandparents. It put a funny lump in his throat.

"Wow, weird, huh?" Doo steered the car with her knee, while she twisted an elastic thing around her hair to make a ponytail. "When I saw those old shacks and stuff? I thought, okay Doo, *now* you've done it. You're gonna end up murdered and buried out in some field for sure! Weren't you, like, nervous?"

Charlie watched until the two old folks shrunk to nothing. "Me? No! She was so nice and so was he. They were just like, I don't know, like neighbors!"

"Whoa, some neighbors!" Doo laughed. "In my neighborhood, people rob you blind and *steal* your car, not fix it! I don't get it . . ."

"Get what?"

"I mean, for nothing? He just fixed the car for nothing. I figured we should get out of there fast, before he changed his mind."

"He wasn't going to change his mind, Doo," said Charlie softly. Didn't she trust anybody?

"How do you know that?"

"Because I know."

"You just ain't been out in the cold, cruel world long enough, Charlie. People don't help you out for nothin'. They just don't."

Charlie was sure she was wrong, but he didn't want to argue about it. The way things were going, it would take days to get to Los Angeles. He didn't want to spend the time arguing. But Doo wasn't going to drive on the highways, and he was beginning to believe it wasn't because she was afraid to.

When they were on the main road again, he asked the question that was sticking in his mind. "How come you lied to them?"

She turned her head quickly and he could see that she was thinking fast. "Well, you don't want them to call the cops, do you? We're just a couple of runaways, you know."

"Well, yeah, I guess. But all that stuff about me being your brother and our folks getting killed . . ." He shook his head. "It just wasn't right."

"Well"—she sniffed—"one of us has to watch out for us, that's for sure."

All Charlie knew for sure was that he was piling up lies as high as John Turner's car-part mountain.

11

They stopped for lunch at Burger Bob's in Shafter.

"My dad will pay you back," said Doo, grabbing the tray filled with burgers, Cokes, and fries. Charlie exchanged a five-dollar bill for forty-three cents in change. Leaving home, he thought $43.75 could take him as far as he needed to go. Now he wasn't so sure.

There was a birthday party going on, so the place was filled with children and balloons. Doo and Charlie watched the noisy party from a two-seater booth. "You got brothers and sisters, Charlie?"

"Two brothers and a sister," he said. "I'm in the middle."

"Why are they getting divorced," she asked, biting into her burger. "Your folks?"

"That's just the thing!" said Charlie. "I don't know!" He sat back, shaking his head. "Don't you think divorced people should ask somebody first? Get permission or something?" The thought came to him in a flash, but the more he thought about it, the better it seemed.

Doo popped a french fry into her mouth. "Permission? From who?"

"I dunno." Charlie shrugged. "From the guy who married them, the pastor of our church. No, *I* know! They should get permission from us! We're the ones who count. We're the family!"

Doo shook her head. "You're a piece of work, Charlie, you know that? You're a real piece of work."

Charlie wasn't sure that was such a good thing to be, a piece of work, so he didn't say any more about his great idea. He asked Doo about her family instead and hoped she wouldn't tell him any more about Manny.

"I got a brother," she said and frowned. "Somewhere. I think he joined the Merchant Marine or something." She'd chewed off all her pink lipstick. Without it, she was sickly pale. But she couldn't be sick, he figured, the way she ate.

"You don't know where your brother is?"

"Nope."

"I bet you miss him, huh?" As often as Charlie wished Tom would leave home, he knew he'd miss him. He knew he'd be sorry to have made such a wish.

"I try not to think about it." She balled up a paper wrapper and tossed it at the trash can, missing.

They sipped their Cokes and joined in when the kids sang "Happy Birthday."

"Well, I had a sister once, too," said Doo, when the party settled down and the kids had their mouths full of birthday cake. "She died."

The lie Doo told John Turner and Norma came back to him. Was she doing it again? "That's too bad," he said, which was all he *could* say.

"She was real little," Doo said sadly. "She was born with this, like, real soft spot on her head?" She touched the top of her own head to show him. "I mostly took care of her 'cause my mom was doing the dry-out thing for her alcohol. If she didn't do it, they said they'd take the baby away. Her name was Pansy."

"The baby? Pansy?"

"Yeah," said Doo, her eyes faraway. "Pansy Jean. Isn't that sweet?"

Charlie said it was. What else could he say? The name Pansy Jean made him feel like cracking up, but he couldn't do that. Not if she was *dead.* "Where was your dad?"

Doo stared at Charlie as if she didn't understand the question. "My dad? He was gone. Somewhere. My folks split up when I was eight."

"Bummer. I bet they didn't ask you first either."

"Not hardly," she muttered. "It was probably Ma's fault, too. She has this, like, temper. They just about took me away from her a couple of times."

"Who?"

"You know. *Them.* The authorities. She took me to

the doctor once because I had this high fever? And the doctor found all these bruises?"

"She beat you?"

"Sure." She shrugged. "Don't you get beat?"

"No! *Never!*"

"I don't get it, Charlie," Doo said, slowly shaking her head. "Why you'd go and take off when you got such a nice family and all."

"Well, that's just it!" Charlie worked hard to make Doo understand, so that he could feel good again about taking off. "It's a *family,* and families belong together."

"Well, even if they split up, you'd still have a family, silly. When it was just Ma and me, it was still a *family.* You don't have to have a mother and a father to have a family."

"I guess not," said Charlie uncertainly. "But it's different."

Doo finished her Coke, rattling the ice in the bottom of the cup. She gazed over at the freckle-faced kid who was opening presents. "I had a birthday party once," she said. "Got me some skates, real skates with white high tops and pink plastic wheels." She looked back at Charlie. "I guess you have lots of parties, huh?"

Charlie, who could have told her about every one of his parties, from the Star Trek party to the camp-out in the backyard just last year, said that, yeah, he'd had a few.

"Got lots of presents, too, I bet."

"Some," he said.

"You got any pets?"

Charlie couldn't help it then. He launched into all the favorite family-pet stories, while she listened like a four-year-old, a look of wonder on her face. "A horse? You got a horse?"

"Well, a pony," he said.

"Wow," said Doo in a soft voice. "I used to want a horse more than anything in the whole world."

"Well, you could still get one," said Charlie. "Someday."

"Yeah, right." Doo smirked. "Someday when I'm about a hundred years old and can't even ride it."

But out in the parking lot she was back to her old self. "Hey, you think you could loan me, like, five bucks?"

Charlie didn't want to be selfish—after all, it was her car and her gas. "Sure," he said, and counted five crumpled dollar bills into Doo's hand.

"Thanks," she said. "I need me some mascara. Mine's all dried up. I'll be right back." She took off across the parking lot toward a string of shops.

Only then did Charlie realize that they'd parked squarely in front of a telephone booth. He tried not to see it as a sign that he should call his folks, but he reached into his pocket and took out a quarter just the same. He turned the dull coin over and over in his fingers. In minutes, no time at all, he could get an operator who would put him through collect to his house, and then *what*?

Carrie would answer, that's what. She *always* answered the telephone. She'd break your arm if you got to it first. Carrie would answer and start screaming at him. He didn't need that. And, besides, Doo was right. He had to wait awhile, at least a couple of days, before he called. That way, they'd know he meant business. Because he did. He meant *business*.

Suddenly a huge wave of homesickness washed over Charlie and he gulped once as if he were drowning. Blinking back tears, he read all the signs in the window of Burger Bob's, twice. Then Doo was back with her mascara and a giant-sized package of Oreo cookies, so life was looking up again as they headed for the next blue road.

12

By late afternoon, Charlie and Doo were in a whole different world, gazing out at the ocean, not ready to believe that they were really there. On glittering yellow sand children played tag and dogs ran free. Boogie-boarders rode the foam of rolling waves onto the beach. Seagulls flew in packs overhead, the older, gray-and-white ones leading, the younger, brown ones at the back. Venice Beach, said a sign on the rail. They were a long, long way from Oakhurst even though it took no time at all to get from there to here.

"You been at the beach much, Charlie?" Somehow Doo had twisted and turned the little car through crowded streets until they came to a street called Ocean Boulevard. She parked the car, they walked three blocks, and there was the ocean. "I bet your folks have a big old summer house right on the water some-wheres, right? And that's where you have all your birthday parties." She looked down at Charlie with a teasing grin. She was chewing a wad of the gum he'd bought them at the minimart, along with Cokes and licorice twists. Sweat beads dotted her nose.

Sure, he'd been to the beach. Not beaches like this one which were full of people and noise and bright colors. The beach Charlie's family knew best was way up in Oregon. It had water too cold to surf without a wet suit, but it was wild and beautiful.

Charlie didn't want to think about family vacations right now. So he just shook his head. "Naw," he said.

Doo flipped her pale yellow hair back from her face. "My dad took me to the beach once. I was real little, like five or six? And he bought me one of those little buckets and a shovel? It was red and I thought I'd died and gone to heaven. It was just him and me . . . But then I didn't see him again." She turned away from the beach and Charlie followed her through the skaters and bicyclers that passed in a parade going both ways at once. "Hey!" she said. "Wanna get some skates?"

Charlie shrugged. "Sure, I guess . . ." He didn't want to tell Doo that he was going to call his folks as soon as he found a pay phone. He'd waited long enough, he decided (even though, two hours before, he'd decided just the opposite). By now, they'd be frantic. They'd tell him to come right home, or else they'd come and get him. They'd have to admit that Charlie was right (even though it wasn't exactly right to run away). They'd say that they were sorry for almost breaking up the family. And everything would be just the way it was before. Perfect.

At the Skate Shack, Charlie shelled out a crumpled twenty-dollar bill. Already he'd bought them hotdogs, two each, and Cokes. After paying to rent the skates, Charlie noted with a sinking heart that he had only a ten, two singles, and some change. "I'll pay you back when we get to my dad's," Doo promised, cradling the shiny plastic skates in her skinny arms.

Charlie saw with relief that she wasn't much better on skates than he was. She pushed along ahead of him like a giant white stork, her bony elbows pumping. He had Carrie to thank for his one skating lesson, but she had been so impatient with his progress that she'd skated off, leaving Charlie to figure things out for himself. And he did, sort of. At least he wasn't falling down as he skidded along behind Doo, flapping his arms like wings. The thing *was*, he told himself, pushing his glasses up his sweaty nose, he hadn't given up. Like his father said all the time, even when it didn't make a whole lot of sense: "There's a lesson in that, son."

After a while, he began to figure it out. If you didn't worry so much about it, about keeping your balance, and you let yourself go free, why, it came real easy. This was a new idea for Charlie, who always thought things through, who took his time and solved problems one step at a time. It felt good to sail along without thinking about it. Then, *womp*, he was on his backside and the world was standing still.

And there, right next to him, was a phone booth. He got unsteadily to his feet and brushed himself off. Rummaging in his pocket for a quarter, he saw that Doo was heading back toward him. He had to laugh at how she seemed to be swimming through the air.

"What happened?" she yelled. "Did you fall?"

He finally got his chance to call home after they returned the skates and Doo set off looking for "a head," as she called it. Charlie raced for the pay phone. With shaking fingers he dug out a quarter and dropped it into the slot. A voice told him how much more to put in, and he was afraid for a second that he wouldn't have enough change. But he did. His stomach was awash with nervous fear and he almost hung up.

"Hello?"

Carrie. No surprise.

"Hi Carrie, it's Charlie."

Carrie let out a piercing shriek. Then she started yelling at him: "Where *are* you? You're such a jerk. You'd better get home right now. Mom and Dad are going crazy! The police were here." Then she gave a blood-curdling yell at the top of her lungs: "*Ma!*"

"Wait!" he cried. "Carrie! Did they read my letter? Are they going to stay together?"

"Is the Pope getting married?"

"Huh?"

"You heard what Dad said. He's moving out."

"Are you sure?"

"You better get home, Charlie. Dad's been driving everywhere, going every place you guys camped. Charlie, where *are* you, anyway?"

In a small voice he said, "They didn't change their minds?"

"Of course not, you dummy. Hang on, I think Ma's next door. Mrs. Patchett made this neat flyer with your picture on it. Wait, I'll go get her."

Charlie heard the phone hit the kitchen table.

Nothing had changed.

He couldn't believe it.

He stared for a minute at the black shiny receiver in his hand. It was slick with his sweat. He reached up and hung it in its cradle.

Doo came up behind him. "So?" she said, in her Doo pose, one hipbone cocked, with a hand propped on it. Charlie chewed on the inside of his cheek for a minute. Then he told her about the call.

"Well, hey." She slapped a hand on his shoulder. "Don't feel bad. They think you don't mean business, that's all. Give 'em some time—" She stopped abruptly and stopped Charlie, too, like a crossing guard, the back of her hand across his chest. "Uh-oh!"

13

Across the stretch of grass that led to the street and Doo's Volkswagen were two black-and-white police cars. There were officers in uniform all over the little yellow car.

"What's going on?" Charlie looked up at Doo's stricken face.

"Come on," she said, hurrying back into the parade of cyclists and skaters. "We'll get our stuff later."

"Huh? What stuff? What's going on, Doo?" Charlie had to hustle to keep up with Doo's long legs.

"Our *stuff*. You know, our clothes and stuff."

Charlie thought about his brand-new backpack, all his gear. His dad would have a fit if something happened to it.

"Why can't we just—?"

But she cut him off. "Oh, Charlie, forget it. That car isn't mine, okay? I just, sort of, you know, borrowed it."

"You stole a car?" Charlie felt paralyzed. He had to stop and take a big gulp of air or stop breathing forever.

But Doo sailed on ahead. "I told you," she said over her shoulder. "I *borrowed* it."

Charlie ran until he caught up with her again. "You mean, like, from a friend or something?"

"Something like that."

"Jeez, Doo!"

"I know, I know," she said.

He wasn't sure what it was she knew. "I'll bet you're sorry now, huh?"

"Huh? Oh, yeah." She plunked down on a bench and crossed her arms over her chest. "I just hope they don't, like, confiscate our things. I've got these neat new jeans and stuff? Damn!"

He had to wonder where she got the "new jeans and stuff" but didn't dare ask. As if a dark cloud had covered the sun, the day that had started off so bright and full of fun dimmed. "I think they have to have a warrant or something," he said glumly. "I read that somewhere."

"Oh, good," she said, relieved. "I didn't think about that." She brightened right up, slapped her palms against her legs, and stood. "They're probably gone by now. Let's sneak back and see."

She was right. The police were gone, but they'd clamped a big lock onto the right front tire. "Come on," Doo cried. "We'll have to be quick." They raced across the grass. While Doo snatched her things out of the back seat, Charlie popped the hood and got his gear. Half of Doo's clothes were in a grocery bag, the rest she piled onto her shoulder. Along with the bag, she carried a huge pink plastic box out of which he'd seen her take her makeup, and a pair of silver shoes with heels so high he was sure a person could never walk in them. "Okay," she said. "Let's find us a bus stop."

Charlie turned back for a last look at the yellow car as they hurried away. He felt as if they were abandoning it. After all, none of this was the car's fault. He'd grown attached to the little Bug with its shiny silver antennae. Attached, he told himself with a stab of guilt, to a *stolen* car! Charlie felt for the first time since leaving home that he was going the wrong way, that he should be walking away from Doo, not alongside her. But what could he do? He couldn't go home, not yet. He didn't even have enough money for bus fare home. He'd have to wait until Doo paid him back. Then he'd figure out what to do.

When the Number 10 bus pulled up, Doo asked the driver how to get to Calaveras Street. Two more buses came and went. Charlie kept looking back to where they'd been, expecting the police to show up any minute and arrest them. Finally, the Number 7 bus pulled up and Doo and Charlie got on.

The bus was full of all kinds of people, all colors, all ages. Some of them laughed and joked with each other or with the bus driver. Some sat and stared off into space. Nobody gave Charlie with his backpack or Doo with her armful of clothes a second glance.

The streets slipped past like a preview of a scary movie. There was graffiti everywhere, most of it in a secret code that Charlie couldn't read. There were spray-paintings of huge ugly people with popping eyes and giant flapping tongues. The farther they traveled, the worse the neighborhoods became, with busted-up sidewalks and trash in the gutters. They passed a huge red brick school surrounded by a high chain-link fence. Behind it, on chewed-up asphalt, boys played basketball, sweat rolling down dark glistening faces. There were broken windows in the school that nobody had bothered to fix, just taped together. On the next block a little boy in a saggy diaper stood in the middle of the sidewalk, crying. Charlie looked for the person the little boy belonged to but saw nobody at all, just the lone little boy bawling his eyes out.

In the seat beside him, Doo went on and on nonstop about her father, about how great he was, about all the things he could do: fly airplanes, hunt for buried treasure, make coins disappear, then pull them out from behind your ear. She didn't have many real stories, not like the ones Charlie could have told if she'd asked about *his* dad. But she didn't ask him about his dad. The closer she came to the address written on the piece of torn-off yellow lined paper she kept in her bra, the more nervous she became and the faster she talked. "Oh!" she cried as the bus made a right turn onto a narrow street lined with old cars, many of them covered with dust, propped up on cinder blocks and missing their wheels. "This is it! Calaveras Street!" She reached up over Charlie and yanked on the bell cord. The bus shooshed to a stop and they got out.

"Maybe he's not here," said Doo in a small, breathless voice as the bus pulled away in a cloud of gray smoke. "I didn't think about that. Like, he's probably at work. Oh!" She stopped dead, her hand over her heart. "There it is. That's his house."

Charlie saw with some relief that the house she pointed to looked pretty good, at least compared to all the others. It was small and needed a good paint job but it had a neat little front porch with potted plants along the rail.

Charlie began to cross the street but Doo held him by the back of his T-shirt. "Wait!" she cried. "Oh, I'm so nervous. What if he doesn't . . . ? I mean, he doesn't know I'm here or nothing . . ."

"Come on," urged Charlie, feeling for a change like the big brother instead of the little one. "He's your dad. He'll be happy to see you." He tugged at her limp hand when she wouldn't move.

They crossed the street and went up a narrow cement walk. On the porch, stacked high as Charlie's head, were old newspapers tied with brown twine. Charlie knocked on the screen door while Doo stood behind him, paler than pale, her green eyes darting everywhere.

"Yes?" A dark face appeared behind the screen, a short person with a dark round face.

Doo's voice came out high and squeaky. "Is my dad here?"

"Your dad?" The face, a woman's face, pushed closer to the screen and stared at Charlie and Doo.

"Jerry Doolittle," Doo said. "My dad."

"Ah." The woman unlocked the door and pushed it open. It screeched just like the one at home and Charlie felt a sharp stab of homesickness. The woman looked Doo up and down, then glanced at Charlie. "Your papa's . . . not here right now." She frowned as if she meant to say something more and changed her mind. On her dress were upside-down and right-side-up red and yellow parrots with keen little eyes. "Come in, come in." She led the way down a narrow hallway lined with photographs in crooked frames, into a tiny kitchen filled with cats. A fluffy orange one in the middle of the kitchen table stretched its back; a striped one stared through slit eyes from the top of the refrigerator. Three kittens slept in a pile under the table, while a white longhair with bright blue eyes yowled by the dinner dish. "He's deaf," the woman said. "Don't mind him. He can't even hear what a racket he's making. *Caramba!*" A tea kettle screamed on the stove and she yanked it off. "I was just crushing cans and making myself a cup of tea. Would you like a Coke or something? Oh," she said and stuck out her hand. "I'm Yolanda. I'm a . . . friend of your daddy's," she said to Doo. "His girlfriend, I guess you could say." Where there weren't cats, there were cans. Aluminum cans, half of them crushed, the other half waiting.

"I'm Doo. This is Charlie," Doo said, leaving the rest to Yolanda's imagination.

Yolanda was short and square with a round tummy in the middle. She had black frizz in a halo all around her face and skin nearly as dark as her hair. Lines fanned out in all directions from her eyes. She wore a gold cross on a chain around her neck with a tiny Jesus on it, and earrings that looked to Charlie like fishing lures.

"Sit down, sit down," she said, and plunked sweating-cold bottles of Coke on the table. "*Dios mio,* it's hot!" She swiped at her forehead with the back of her hand. The orange cat rolled over to have its belly scratched, then closed its eyes and went to sleep, all four paws in the air. Thirsty and tired, Charlie chugged down half his drink. "Now tell me how you got here, you two." Yolanda leaned against the stove, her arms crossed over the parrots on her dress.

Without batting an eye, Doo told a rambling story about all the buses she'd had to take from Sacramento. Nothing about the little yellow car or Manny, the stepfather. Then she seemed to remember that she had to account for Charlie somehow, so she said she'd met him in a bus station. "He's running away," she explained. "But just until his folks get back together."

"I see," said Yolanda, frowning, but she didn't. He

could tell that she wanted to call his folks right that minute, and that if she knew his last name or telephone number, she would.

He vowed not to tell her either one, not if she tortured him.

She didn't look like the torturing kind.

"You're hungry, no?" she said. She reopened the small refrigerator and took out a jar of mayonnaise and a package of bologna. "Kids are always hungry. And I suppose you need a place to stay, too, right?"

"Will my dad be back soon?" Doo sat on the edge of her chair, her bony shoulders hunched.

Yolanda's back was to them while she made their sandwiches. The kitchen got extra quiet. Even the deaf white cat stopped its yowling.

"Yolanda?" Doo's voice went up the scale.

Yolanda lifted her hands and said something to the ceiling that Charlie couldn't hear. She turned. She sighed deeply. "Well," she said, this time just to Doo, "let me put it this way. Your daddy won't be back for a while." The white cat threaded itself in and out of her legs.

"How long?" Doo looked frightened, as if she knew something wasn't right.

"Oh, *hija*," Yolanda said, and sat herself down like a heavy sack of flour. "Your papa's in jail. Didn't you know that?"

14

When Charlie woke up with his sleeping bag over his face, he thought at first he was back in the woods. Then he felt the hard floor beneath him and remembered where he was, Yolanda's living room. He got up and rolled his bag so that it would stuff neatly into its sack. In the kitchen he could hear Yolanda's voice and the yowl of the white cat.

When he came into the kitchen, he saw Yolanda piling cookies into a shoebox. "This what you're going to show your papa?" she said to Doo. "This face?"

Doo blinked.

"Good morning, Charlie," said Yolanda. "Get yourself a bowl of cereal. Milk's in the fridge. I was just telling Doo here that it's not exactly a picnic in jail. Her papa's gonna need cheering up."

Doo sat with her knees drawn up and her arms wrapped around them. Her underpants showed but she didn't seem to care. She stared glumly across the kitchen at the dripping faucet, chin on her knees.

Charlie wondered why she never asked Yolanda what her father was doing in jail. She didn't even act surprised. Charlie had plenty of questions but he knew it wasn't his place to ask them. Maybe he would ask Doo later, or maybe she would just tell him. Was her father a bank robber? a dope dealer? a *murderer?* Maybe he stole a car. Maybe stealing just ran in the family or something. Charlie watched Doo's face, waited for her to say something, *anything.* He felt sorry for her and tried to think of the right words to tell her what he felt without making her feel worse.

Would he be looking for the right words all his life? Did it ever get easier? He thought maybe the right words just started tumbling around in your brain when you were a teenager. But Carrie didn't have the right words and neither did Tom. Even Charlie's father was having trouble finding them now and he was a grownup.

Charlie ate his cereal and thought about how his life would be if *his* father got put in jail. But he couldn't imagine something like that happening to his father. It would have to be a mistake. Still, Charlie knew how terrible his father would feel. How terrible the whole family would feel. At school the kids would all know. They'd say mean things or else just look away, and he'd feel ashamed.

That was the worst thing, he thought: he'd be ashamed of his own father. He'd carry the shame around, even though he was just a kid. It would follow him like his shadow and become his own shame.

"And you," Yolanda said, "Charlie!" Charlie jumped. "You said you wanted to come along to the jail, but I'm not taking two sad sacks, no way! Now you two go get cleaned up."

Doo sighed. She unfolded herself and stood.

"Wear something pretty," Yolanda ordered. "Let her use the bathroom first, Charlie. Girls take forever."

Charlie felt her eyes on him as he finished his breakfast. "How old are you, Charlie?" she said. "If you don't mind me askin'."

Charlie's spoon stopped halfway to his mouth. "Uh . . ."

He just couldn't do it. He couldn't break the trustworthy law, not twice in two days.

"Eleven," Charlie muttered into his cookie.

Yolanda slid out a chair and sat down. She laid her brown arms on the table and waited for Charlie to look up. "You been in foster care?"

"No, ma'am. At least I don't think so. What is it?"

"Well, it's a place for kids who need homes and parents, somebody to watch over them because their families can't. Or won't."

"Oh, no, ma'am," Charlie said, relieved. "My folks are great. I mean, they'd never put us in foster care. My ma would *die* first!"

"Then what are you doing with Jerry's dau . . . with Doo?"

"It just . . . happened," Charlie said, surprised all over again as he thought about it. "I was eating this doughnut and Doo came in and . . ."

Yolanda looked puzzled.

"I was running away from home," Charlie said. "Sort of."

"*Sort* of."

"Well, not really. I didn't mean to get this far. I'm going home. Soon as my folks change their minds about getting a divorce."

"Oh," said Yolanda. He thought he saw a tiny smile start up at the corners of her mouth, but how could that be? Divorce wasn't anything to smile about. "Would tomorrow morning be a good time?"

"Maybe," said Charlie. "I'd have to phone them."

"Why don't you do that right now."

He told her about the call he'd made just the day before.

"Charlie," Yolanda said very seriously, the way teachers talked to real little kids, first-graders. Charlie wasn't liking that much. "I think you should just go on home anyway, no matter what happens. Your folks are going to do what they're going to do. You know that, don't you?"

Charlie wasn't sure, so he didn't answer.

"What if you got your wish? What if they stayed together just for you but they weren't happy? You wouldn't want that, would you?"

Charlie thought a minute. "No, ma'am, but—"

"But what?"

"They *were* happy." Saying the words and hearing them, Charlie knew suddenly how true they were. They'd been happy once, but they weren't anymore. It had been a long time since he'd heard his mother sing, since his father laughed and joked around. He remembered the way his dad used to pat his mother's butt when she walked past his chair. How she would swat his hand away and how they'd both laugh and get embarrassed if any of the kids were watching. His dad always kissed his mom before he went off to work, every time. Once when he forgot, he came driving all the way back from Four Corners just to get the job done. His father could make his mother's eyes get all fuzzy-looking. But he hadn't done that in a long time either.

How long? Charlie couldn't remember.

"How about I call your folks," Yolanda said. "You get a good night's sleep, and I'll put you on the Greyhound in the morning."

Charlie looked away from her concerned eyes. He liked Yolanda and he wanted her to like him, to see how serious he was about fixing his family. But he wasn't ready to go home, to give in.

He could see she wouldn't give in either, so he nodded his head. "Okay," he said.

"I'll call them when we get back," Yolanda said. "Now go bang on the bathroom door and tell that girl not to run the shower forever."

Charlie left the kitchen thinking there was something he didn't tell Yolanda, not because he didn't want to tell her but because the thought was so new he hadn't yet told himself. It was a scary thought, kind of, and so he'd kept it tucked way down in the cellar of his brain. If he let it out and looked at it, he wasn't sure he was going to like it, or like himself for thinking it.

The thing was, Charlie knew now, he'd left home for two reasons. The first was the most important and that hadn't changed. Somebody had to do something to make Mom and Dad wake up. It was kind of like a good deed, a really big good deed, if he could save his family from being broken.

The other reason was different and it was the one he wasn't as proud of. Charlie was just a little sick and tired of being good, of being Mister Sunshine. He was growing up but nobody at home seemed to know that. They all looked over the top of his head as if he wasn't there. They all expected him to behave and not cause trouble, when everybody else did—even his grownup parents!

Out here in the *real* world, he could be anybody he wanted to be. And Doo treated him like a real person, pretty much. Not just because she thought he was thirteen either, at least he didn't think so.

He was having fun. He was even going to go inside a real live jail.

15

On the Number 19 bus Doo painted her fingernails. Green this time. Her eyes were puffy and pinkish-looking and she still hadn't said much, just yes and no and, when she remembered, thank you and please.

Yolanda sat with the box of cookies on her lap. She'd changed the parrot dress for a dark blue one with a lace collar, a Sunday-school-teacher dress, and her hair was captured in a clip at the back of her neck. Charlie watched the scenery go by and tried to remember landmarks, the way a good Scout would, in case he had to find his own way back.

The bus stopped a hundred times and, each time, Charlie looked out the window for a jail. He thought they'd never get there. At last, Yolanda got up out of her seat and headed down the aisle, rocking back and forth as the bus eased to a stop. Charlie and Doo followed behind.

On the sidewalk, which was filled with people passing both ways, Charlie looked for a sign that said "Jail" or for some barred windows to let people know where the jail was, but all he saw was a regular-looking building, like a bank.

"Here we are," Yolanda said and headed for the building. 150—POLICE DEPARTMENT—CITY OF LOS ANGELES it said over the entrance, which made Charlie's knees turn to water.

Inside, the air was cool and dusty. Charlie took off his cowboy hat. Their footsteps echoed across the marble floor. Charlie's heart hammered in his ears. What if somebody made a mistake and he got locked inside? And then he just got forgotten for about a hundred years and only his bones (and his glasses and the red cowboy hat) were found later, when they got around to remembering.

His glasses slid down his sweaty nose and when he pushed them back into place they were fogged with his nervous breath.

Charlie was all ready to say he was Doo's cousin, that Jerry Doolittle was his uncle, even though he'd be breaking the first Scout law again. You had to be family to visit an inmate. He thought about the way one lie kind of led to another. The Boy Scout manual was right about that.

They got into an elevator filled with people who didn't seem a bit worried that they were all going down into the basement. When the elevator stopped with a thump, Doo and Charlie followed Yolanda, who followed the others down a narrow hallway. They came to a stop at a huge iron gate.

Standing at the head of the short line of people were two guards in brown uniforms with guns belted on. Charlie hoped the guards checked the prisoners as carefully as they were checking the visitors. He hoped the prisoners didn't pick today to start a riot. Charlie didn't want to be a hostage. He didn't think there was a merit badge for demonstrating survival techniques or showing Scout spirit in a jail cell.

He tried to keep his nervous hands still. He kept them out of his pockets in case anyone thought he was carrying *contraband.*

Doo sighed a lot, as if she couldn't catch her breath, and picked at the polish she'd just put on. "Hey, cuz," she said softly. He glanced up and saw her grinning down at him. "You okay?"

He nodded, even though he was about to swallow his lying tongue.

And Doo? Did she make up *all* those stories about her father? Did he really fly a plane and hunt for buried treasure?

Close up, the guards were eight feet tall, and Charlie figured they'd have to be pretty mean or they wouldn't be guards. So he was surprised when the one that opened Yolanda's shoebox laughed and pretended he was going to steal some of the cookies. "You keep your hands off them cookies, Harold," Yolanda warned. Harold took the cookies and promised Doo's father would get them.

The other guard had a metal detector wand, the kind they used in airports, and he was going up and down the visitors with it. Charlie beeped when they went over him and his heart nearly stopped. Everybody got real quiet, even though he was only a kid. *Beep* went the wand and the guard asked Charlie to empty his pockets. Only then did Charlie remember his knife. Shamefaced, he took it out of his pocket and handed it over. He hoped the guard didn't think he'd brought the knife on purpose, that he was going to slip it to Doo's father, that he was one of the *bad* people.

A huge gate slid open and Charlie went with the crowd through it. It slammed closed with a metallic clang and he nearly jumped out of his boots. They stopped at a regular door with a chicken-wire window in it. A few of the visitors went through; the rest waited.

"It won't be too long," promised Yolanda.

Finally, it was their turn.

The door opened and Doo and Charlie followed Yolanda into half a room. It had green-painted walls with nothing on them, not even a light switch. To their left was a long counter and low stools. They sat down facing a big window. On the other side of the window was the other half of the room. It had yellow cinder-block walls and nothing else. "Where's my dad?" whispered Doo, her eyes wide.

"Wait just a minute, sweetie," said Yolanda, patting Doo's hand. Just as she said, "He's coming," out came a guard, and behind him, a small skinny man wearing a green doctor's suit (the kind of suit the doctor wore to take out Charlie's tonsils). Jerry Doolittle was a lot older than Charlie thought he would be, older than Charlie's dad, who was mostly bald even though he wasn't old enough to be. Doo's father had some gray fuzz around his ears and the dome of his head gleamed in the fluorescent lights. His face was full of wrinkles but, unlike Yolanda's, all the wrinkles went down. He looked straight into Yolanda's eyes and gave her a sad smile. Then he reached for the telephone, and Yolanda reached for the one on their side. Charlie and Doo could hear Yolanda but could only watch Doo's father's lips moving.

"Got a surprise for you, Jerry," Yolanda said.

Doo's dad's eyebrows went up a little.

"This big girl here." Yolanda reached over and pulled Doo under her arm and Doo was looking at her father for the first time since she was six. "This here's your daughter, Doo."

Charlie could easily read Jerry Doolittle's lips: "You're kidding!"

Yolanda handed Doo the telephone.

"Daddy?" And then she started to cry. She held her hand over her mouth to hold back her sobs and tried to talk in between them. "Daddy, when are you getting out?"

Doo's daddy hung his head as he talked, so Charlie couldn't tell what he was saying. Every once in a while, Doo would answer, "Uh-huh, uh-huh." After a while she said, "Can I come and live with you then?"

Doo's dad got very excited. He started talking a mile a minute, too fast for Charlie to make out what he was saying, but he seemed to be painting pictures in the air with his free hand.

They talked for a little while longer. Then Doo handed the phone to Yolanda. "He wants to talk to you," she said. Her whole body went into a slump.

"Did he say you could live with him later? When he gets out?"

"Oh, sure," Doo said bitterly. "He says we'll get this *big* house, and I'll have my *own* room and TV and a Princess phone—get that? *Princess* phone! A car, too." She shook her head. "Yeah, *right* . . ."

"Wow," said Charlie. "Maybe he means it."

"Sure, he *means* it. He just won't *do* it. That much I know about him."

"But *how* do you know? Maybe he's changed now. Maybe he learned his lesson in there." He and Doo looked past Yolanda at the cinder-block walls, at the guard standing at attention by the door, hands clasped behind his back, his gun visible in a big black belt on his hip. "I mean, a person would have a chance to really think about things and—"

"Oh, Charlie"—Doo sighed—"just shut up, will you?"

So he did. For a while.

Then he couldn't help himself. "Did you tell him about, you know, how it was with Manny?"

She stared at him for a minute as if she didn't know what he was talking about. "Are you kidding?" Then: "Nah, he can't do nothin'."

Charlie guessed that she was right. But then he thought maybe knowing about Manny would make Doo's dad try harder to get out. Maybe he wasn't as good as he could be in there. Maybe he could be better.

Then Charlie remembered what she had said about "fixing things" before she left home. Whatever that meant. She probably didn't want her daddy to know about that.

Charlie looked at Doo in her flowery dress and her ten ear studs and thought there was an awful lot about her that he didn't really know.

Doo's father turned and looked over his shoulder at the guard by the door. He said something to Yolanda and she said, "Damn. Well, okay then." She said something in Spanish, something that sounded like a love poem. Doo's dad smiled. He reached up and put his hand against the glass, fingers spread like octopus tentacles. Yolanda put her hand over his. Charlie could see by their wet eyes that they loved each other. Maybe Jerry Doolittle would get out and marry Yolanda, and then Yolanda could be Doo's mom, well, stepmom . . . Charlie's mind raced ahead, making big plans for Doo's life.

Yolanda removed her hand from the glass, but Doo's dad kept his right where it was. He looked with big hopeful eyes at Doo. But Doo just stood with her hands clasped behind her back, so tight the blood had left her fingers, and stared at the floor.

"Go ahead, honey," encouraged Yolanda, but Doo turned away and ran toward the door.

Charlie, feeling sorry for Doo's dad, turned and waved. Doo's dad gave Charlie a sad grin and waved back.

Once they had gotten through the big iron gate, Yolanda and Charlie had a hard time keeping up with Doo. She stalked ahead with her long legs and silver shoes and never once looked back.

They caught up with her outside. She waited impatiently, arms crossed over her chest, her eyes red from crying. But she didn't look sad anymore, she looked angry.

"Here comes the bus," said Yolanda. "Right on time for a change." She hurried toward the bus stop, but just as Charlie started to follow, Doo grabbed his arm. "Come on," she hissed.

"But—"

"I said, come on!" She took off at a run. Charlie stood between Yolanda running for the bus and Doo running for . . . what? He didn't know, but he knew he had to catch her. He had to tell her what could happen in the future if she just stopped and thought about it for a minute. He took off after her, but she was moving fast, dodging in and out of pedestrians, crossing the street against the light.

"*Charl-i-e!*"

He looked up as the bus zoomed past. Yolanda's head was stuck out the bus window. "Take the next bus!" she yelled. "The Number 8!"

16

Keeping Doo in sight, Charlie ran for all he was worth. She was quick, even in her high-heeled shoes. She dodged in and out of people and it was hard to see her sometimes.

Once, he thought he'd lost her and he stopped. The city swirled around him in a kaleidoscope of color and light, with honking horns and screeching brakes and air he couldn't breathe. Sick and dizzy, he realized right then that all he had to do was call his folks and they would come to get him. Spotting a flag of yellow hair in the distance, he took off again. At last he caught up. Doo was leaning against a light pole, bent over, trying to get her breath back.

Charlie dropped down onto the curb, breathing hard.

"I wish I never saw him!" Doo cried and kicked a

mailbox with her silver shoe. "He's just a jerk. A con!"

Charlie remembered the sad look in Jerry Doolittle's eyes as he watched his daughter walk away from him. "But he loves you, Doo," he said.

Doo groaned. "Sometimes, Charlie, you sound about eleven years old, you know?" She folded herself down and sat beside him on the curb. Her stringy blond hair fell forward, hiding her face. "He doesn't love me. He doesn't even know me."

"But you're his daughter. He has to love you. Besides, I could see it in his eyes."

Doo turned to Charlie with a smirk on her face. "Give me a break! You could *see* it . . . ! What did it look like? A pink heart? With, like, lace or something? You could *see* it . . ." She rolled her eyes.

"I *could*," Charlie insisted. "You can see love." Then he was embarrassed and looked down at his boots, appreciating his father so much all at once that a big fat lump came into his throat.

They sat side by side on the curb as the traffic zipped past, Doo in her flowered dress, Charlie in his hiking boots and dirty jeans and red cowboy hat. "Yolanda said to take the Number 8," Charlie said after a while.

Doo picked at a smooshed piece of bright pink gum that was stuck to the bottom of her shoe. "I don't want to go back to Yolanda's," she said.

"Why not? She's nice."

Where else could they go?

"Yolanda could be your stepmom someday. That would be cool . . ."

"*If* my old man ever gets out. Like I should count on *that*!"

A golden retriever came padding up, sniffed Charlie's face, and gave him a big wet kiss.

"Whoa!" Doo laughed. She and Charlie petted the dog all over while he wriggled happily. Then, hearing a far-off whistle, he took off like a shot.

"There," said Charlie. "Did you see that?"

"What?"

"In the dog's eyes!"

"*What?*"

"Love!"

Doo wrapped her long arms around her legs and laid her chin on her knees. "Love's only in the movies," she muttered. "That's where the happy-ever-after stuff is, too. The sooner you figure that out, kiddo, the better off you'll be. Come on." She sighed, getting up and brushing off her dress.

"Where are we going?"

"Back to the beach."

Charlie argued that they should go to Yolanda's first and get their stuff and then go to the beach. Once he got Doo there, he would call his folks, but he didn't tell her that part.

"Maybe later," she said. "I've got to think." She stalked off and he followed.

Along the way, she asked three bus drivers how to get to Venice Beach and finally found the right bus. "You got any money, Charlie?" she said, halfway up the bus steps. He pulled out the last of his $43.75, a sorry little bunch of crumpled-up dollar bills.

"I thought my dad would give me some, you know, *money!*" she said when they were seated and the bus zoomed away from the curb. Her laugh was bitter. "He was, like, in a cage! God! I just want to get as far away from him as I can. I don't even want to think about him anymore."

"Doo?"

She didn't answer at first. She was staring out the window, sucked deep into her own thoughts.

"Doo?"

She turned and looked at him and Charlie saw right then that he was her friend. He saw it in her eyes. It made him happy, but it scared him at the same time. He never knew what she might do, yet if he was her friend, he'd be a part of whatever that was. It was up to him to show her there were better ways of doing things than the way she sometimes did them. But would she listen to him?

"You could come stay with us," he said. "With my mom and us."

She grinned, but he could see she wasn't taking him seriously.

"You *could*," he insisted. "We have a big old farm-house, really big. You could share Carrie's room." He got a sudden vision of Carrie's angry face with the pink octopus telephone stuck to her ear. Who was he kidding? Carrie wouldn't share her room with anybody.

"So you *are* a rich kid. I figured . . ."

"Nah, we're not rich. My mom grows most of our food and my dad's a teacher. They argue about money all the time. Maybe it's why they're getting a divorce. I don't know . . ."

"Then just what they need is another kid," she said.

Charlie stared out at the city as it passed the dirty bus windows. Both his heart and his head told him that he and Doo were going the wrong way, and the farther they went, the surer he was. He turned his head to look at the faces of the passengers all around him. They were people he didn't know and would never know. Strangers. Strangers didn't care what happened to him, they had their own troubles, their own kids to worry about. He began to be afraid, really afraid, as if a part of him knew that he and Doo were headed for the worst trouble yet.

Beside him, Doo, cracking her gum, was caught up in her own sad thoughts. Charlie was on his own, *really* on his own. It was like the time he'd gotten on the wrong ride at the local fair, thanks to Carrie, who should have known better. The ride went through a dark tunnel that was full of terrible nightmare things that jumped out from the walls or dangled in his face. There were howls and screeches and dead ends, and Charlie had nightmares for weeks afterward.

He felt like that now, like he'd gotten on the wrong ride, way back when Doo screeched out of the dough-nut shop parking lot, heading south.

At Ocean Boulevard, they got off the bus and began making their way toward the beach. The closer they got, the happier Doo became. "I like it down here," she said. "It makes me feel, I don't know"—she threw her hands in the air—"*free*! Look over there!" She pointed to a square of dried yellow grass that was full of peo-ple, mostly old men, lying around. "If you had your tent we could put it up right over there in the middle of that grass." When they got closer, Charlie could see that the men all had too many clothes on for the beach, raggedy jackets over dirty shirts and pants with rips and tears in them. They were sipping from a bottle wrapped in a brown paper bag and passing it around.

"Hey, girlie!" called one of the men, waving the bot-tle. "Wanna party?"

Doo pretended not to hear.

"Doo?"

"Yeah?"

"I don't like it here. Let's go."

"Charlie?"

"Yeah?"

"How old do you think I am?"

"I dunno. Sixteen?"

"Yeah? You really think I look sixteen?"

"I guess . . ."

"Well, I'm fourteen." She flipped her yellow hair over her shoulder. "I *look* sixteen, though!"

"You can't be fourteen!" Charlie protested. "You drive a car."

"Yeah, I know," she said. "Manny taught me how. So's I could run errands for him and Ma, like buy them cigs and stuff?"

"But you can't even buy cigarettes!"

"Wanna bet?"

Did she *ever* tell the truth?

A swarm of strange people passed, people with strange hairstyles and funny clothes. Some had more tattoos than clothes. A little girl with a skinny yellow dog held out her hand and begged for change, while a baldheaded lady wandered in circles, talking to the sky. They passed a children's playground that looked like a big cage. On the gate was a sign: ADULTS WITHOUT CHILDREN NOT ALLOWED INSIDE. Grownups couldn't be trusted here. It didn't seem right, but there it was on the sign.

Strolling along beside him, Doo giggled at the strange people. Soon she'd left the last bits of her sadness behind. Which was good and not so good. Charlie didn't want Doo to feel bad, but how was he ever going to get her back to Yolanda's if she was happy here?

"Doo?"

"Yeah?"

"Where are we going to stay, if we don't go back to Yolanda's?" The sun had begun to set and families were coming up from the beach, carrying their umbrellas and coolers, going home, where it was safe. Going home to places they would never think of running away from. Soon it would be just him and Doo and the others who seemed to live right here on the streets. What if he and Doo ended up here? Living on the streets . . . for *good!* "Let's go back to Yolanda's," he urged, hearing the panic in his voice and not even caring that it was there.

"We just got here!" she said.

"Aren't you hungry?"

"A little. Don't worry. We can find something. People throw out perfectly good food all the time."

Charlie's stomach rolled over. "Yuck!"

"Hey, it's food," she said. "Don't be so picky!" She stopped at a trash barrel and began poking through it.

Charlie kept on walking, pretending he didn't even know the strange girl going through the trash cans. *Homeless,* he said to himself. *Homeless.* It was just a word before, and not even a very bad one. Homeless always happened to other people, not to families he knew, not to kids like him. Now he wasn't so sure that it couldn't happen to just anybody.

"Look!" Doo cried, catching up. "Almost a whole hamburger!" She chomped into it and handed it, half wrapped in yellow paper, over to Charlie.

"You can have it," he said, his stomach heaving.

"Suit yourself. It's good. Not too much sauce." She took a big fat bite and chewed it happily.

The sun melted like a blob of orange sherbet into a silvery blue sea. There were fewer people on the sidewalks now, black cut-out silouettes against the fading light. Charlie walked with his hat pulled down and his arms crossed. Doo knew he didn't want to be here, but she didn't seem to care. And if she didn't care, why should he?

But he did care. He cared about her. He couldn't seem to help it.

17

From a distance came the soft strumming of a guitar. Doo began to hum along with it. And then she was making her way toward the music, across the wide sidewalk, Charlie hurrying along to keep up with her.

If there was a word for Doo, Charlie thought, it would probably be *slippery*. You never knew what she was going to do next.

On a bench along the railing was a guitar player, a man dressed all in black. Charlie saw by his hands and by his face when he looked up from under his black hat that he was a black man. If it weren't for the sound of his guitar, they might not have found him in the darkness.

"Good evening," he said politely and laid his guitar across his knees.

"Good evening," said Charlie in the same polite way.

"Hi," said Doo.

"Y'all are out pretty late. It's suppertime." He smiled, and his eyes and teeth glowed. "I can hear your mamas calling you." He laughed softly to himself. "Here, have a seat." He upended his guitar and leaned it against his legs so that they could sit beside him on the bench, one on either side. As soon as he sat down, Charlie could feel how tired he was. Something about the guitar player made him feel safe. He wanted to trust that feeling. He wanted to lay his head against the big man's shoulder and close his eyes, but of course he couldn't.

"Name's Jason," the man said, turning first to Doo, then to Charlie, extending a big calloused hand. "You two just visiting for the day? Ain't seen you 'round here."

"We're visiting our aunt," Doo said without a second thought. "Our Aunt Yolanda."

"I'm Charlie," Charlie said before Doo could tell another lie. "This is Doo."

Doo gave Charlie a disgusted look.

"Well, Doo . . . Charlie . . . happy to meet you. I'll sing you a tune. Would you like that?"

An open guitar case at the man's feet held some dollar bills and a scattering of change. "That's okay," said Charlie, who figured they had to give the man some money, which they hardly had.

But Doo asked right away, "Can you play 'Somewhere Over the Rainbow'?"

"I can try," said Jason and took up his guitar. He

strummed a few chords, then reached down into his case for something that he clamped over the skinny end. Then he began to play the famous song.

When Doo began to sing, Charlie felt his jaw drop open. She sounded like an angel, she sounded even better than the girl who sang the song in the movie. Never before did Charlie think that a song could be so sad and so hopeful all at the same time. Her voice gave him goosebumps.

"Now, that was truly fine!" said Jason when she'd finished. "You are one talented young lady. Better not set up shop around here." He laughed. "You'll put me out of business!"

"I didn't know you could sing!" said Charlie, his heart still ringing with the last sad words and her voice as it rose with the bluebirds to the final high note.

"You don't know everything about me!" Doo said, but she looked pleased and proud.

"That's for sure," Charlie grumbled, but mostly to himself.

Then Jason and Doo sang some songs together. Jason encouraged Charlie to join in, but Charlie just shook his head. He knew he'd just ruin how good they sounded together. A small crowd gathered, a couple arm in arm, and two kids wearing black heavy-metal T-shirts. The couple wandered off after a while, but then the girl hurried back and dropped some change into Jason's guitar case.

"I do thank you kindly!" Jason said. Then he turned

to the two boys who were left. "Shep, you still hanging out? Didn't you move in with your big brother?"

Shep shrugged. "Yeah. Sorta."

"And who's your pal here?"

The boy named Shep was tall and blond and skinny as a scarecrow. His friend was short with dark scruffy hair. He stood with his shoulders hunched forward, hands stuffed down into low-slung jeans. He looked like he'd had a real bad day, maybe lots of them. When Shep introduced him as Joel, he didn't take his hand out of his pocket to shake Jason's. Jason shrugged, looked down at his guitar, and strummed a few notes. "This here's Doo and Charlie," he said. "They just stopped by on their way home to dinner. Ain't that right?" Jason looked at Charlie as if to say they'd *better* be going home to dinner, and all at once Charlie felt that Jason knew all about him and Doo without them even telling him one true thing except their names.

Charlie didn't know what to say. All of a sudden he wanted to tell Jason everything, every crazy thing that had happened since he left home. He wanted to stop worrying about Doo and about himself and his family. He wanted to lay all his problems in the big man's guitar case so he could be just a kid again. *Blueberry, swoon, scalawag . . .*

Shep said hi.

Joel grunted.

After a while, Jason stood up and stretched. "Well,

y'all better go on your way," he said. "It's gettin' late." He leaned over and started gathering up his change.

"Hey, Jason?" It was Shep.

"Yeah, kid?"

"You think you could, like, give us a loan, me and Joel? Just a couple bucks for a burger."

Jason stood up and frowned. He was the tallest, blackest man Charlie had ever been close to and he wondered why he felt so safe when he was just a stranger. "You know I can't do that, son," said Jason. "I give to you, and a dozen more just like you show up tomorrow. Like a pack of crows. This is the way I make my living, you know that. Now get along with you."

He laid his guitar in the case. He closed and snapped the lid. The two boys took off. Charlie heard the shorter one, Joel, complaining to Shep about how he'd promised something and now . . .

Jason set off, his guitar case in one hand, bedroll in the other. "Get along home to your aunt now, you two," he said. "Thanks for the sweet song!"

Doo and Charlie wandered along behind Jason in silence, but he gained on them, finally disappearing into the darkness. Charlie wondered where Jason was going and, if he and Doo had to sleep outside all night, if they could sleep next to him.

18

They wandered farther along the dark boulevard, past bars spewing smoke and smelling of spilled beer. Two bare-chested boys on skateboards slalomed past, cutting close, their bodies curving inward like commas. "Yeee-oow!" yelled one, and the other answered, "Yowza!"—their voices echoing into the dark.

Charlie stuffed his hands into his pockets and walked with his head down.

"What's wrong, Charlie? You homesick or something?"

"I guess . . ." he said. She'd been chattering about nothing, about dumb things she used to do with her friends in fourth grade. Charlie hadn't said a thing. He'd been looking into the face of the pale white moon, the same moon that had lighted his way down the dirt road away from his house. It seemed so long ago.

"Lighten up, cuz. We'll find you some dinner, don't worry. And a place to sleep, too. Anyway, you're a Boy Scout. You should know what to do!"

Charlie thought how different it was in the woods. You knew there were bears and stuff. You wore a bear bell to warn them away and you knew what to do if you saw one on the trail. Here you had to be ready for anything, for things you didn't even know about. Adults who didn't act like adults and who couldn't be trusted around children. He wished they'd followed Jason, or gone back to Yolanda's. Anywhere but here. He couldn't shake the feeling that something bad was going to happen in this place.

"Guess what I see?" said Doo suddenly. Charlie, walking with his head down, his hands stuffed into his pockets, looked up and saw it, too. Wendy's Donuts. Like the shop at Four Corners, it lit the whole world up.

Inside were racks and racks of doughnuts: glazed, raised, strawberry-sprinkled, cinnamon twists. Doughnut heaven. Charlie's spirits lifted. He took out his remaining two dollar bills and seventy-six cents in change.

"Go ahead," Doo urged. "Get one."

"Nah," said Charlie, staring at a chocolate-covered cream. He knew it was dumb, a doughnut couldn't fix anything, but if he could just have one gushy bite of that chocolate-covered cream, he almost believed that his fears would melt away.

Maybe.

At least for a little while.

"I just want coffee," Doo said.

How could that be, with all these doughnuts staring at her? But when he looked up, she nodded emphatically. "Just coffee."

"One chocolate-cream doughnut and one coffee," he told the girl behind the counter.

"This is just like where we first met, huh, Charlie? Jeez, I sure miss my jacket and my green skirt."

"And your makeup case," he added, so it would sink in and she would agree to go back to Yolanda's.

They sat in a booth like the one at Four Corners. The chocolate-covered doughnut on its perfect little square of waxed paper looked too good to eat. Charlie stared at it. It was as if, once his favorite food in all the world was gone, he might never ever taste it again for the rest of his life.

Doo was staring at it, too.

"It's your favorite kind, too, isn't it?"

She tried to shrug it off, sipping her hot coffee, but Charlie could see that he'd guessed right.

He took out his pocket knife and very carefully, as if it was the most important thing he would ever do, he cut the doughnut in half.

Doo shared her coffee.

"I like being on the road with you, Charlie," Doo said. "You bug me sometimes but, like, I never had a little brother or nothin'." She bit into the doughnut.

Thought hard about something. " 'Course, you already got a big sister." She licked chocolate off her lips and the tips of her fingers. Frowned. "I guess you're ready to go home, huh?"

"Yeah," he said, relieved that he didn't have to say it first. "As soon as we go back to—"

"I know," she said, "I *know*"—waving her hand to shut him up. But Charlie couldn't tell if that meant she would go, or that she wouldn't.

"I did a really bad thing," she said after a while, biting her lip. "I mean, *really* bad. I didn't want to tell you before because, well, I figured you wouldn't hang out with me no more if I did."

"What?" Charlie's heart cartwheeled. What could be worse than stealing a car? "What did you do?"

She bent her plastic coffee stirrer in half, then in fourths. She frowned. She wouldn't look at him. "I set the house on fire."

"You *what?*" A hand squeezed Charlie's stomach like a sponge.

"Before I left? While Manny was sleeping? I got all this newspaper and stuff? And I just . . . just lit it."

"Doo!" Charlie stared at Doo, wide-eyed. Her little angel earring was turned on its head.

"My ma was at work. She works the night shift cleaning floors at this, like, mental hospital? I wouldn't want to hurt her or nothin'. But *him!*" She shook her head.

"What happened? Did the house burn down?" Charlie had nightmarish visions of a man on fire running from a burning house. "Did Manny . . . ? Did you . . . ?"

She shrugged. "I dunno. That's when I took off. I knew that the kid next door always left his keys in his car. I went for a ride with him once and I saw him just pop them under the mat after. Like nobody would think to look for them there. So"—she shrugged again—"I took it."

"The yellow Bug."

She sighed. "I guess he's got it back now. Maybe he learned a lesson about leaving his keys in the car. Maybe I, like, did him a *favor.*"

Was she kidding?

She told him about grabbing up all the things she could think to take with her. About being panicked when she couldn't find her pink makeup case. Charlie just kept thinking about Manny burning up. "Why did you hate him so much? Did he beat you?"

"Worse," she said. She looked at Charlie then like the little boy he was, and seemed to change her mind about what she was going to say. "He did *things* . . . things a father, or a stepfather, or any grownup man should never do to a girl." She bit her lip. "You don't want to hear about it."

"Did your mom know?"

She looked about to cry but blinked back her tears. She was really good at that when she wanted to be. "Yeah," she said, and slumped back against the booth.

"She knew. She said she didn't believe me. That I was just trying to steal her boyfriend."

Charlie felt sick inside. "Why didn't you tell somebody else? Why didn't you go live somewhere else? With an aunt or somebody . . ."

"I been in and out of places," Doo said. "My ma was in jail, too, you know, for a while. Prison." Doo scooped out a fly that was swimming in her coffee and shook it onto the table. The fly did scissor kicks in the air, then righted itself and flew off. "You know what my daddy's in for, Charlie? He didn't have to tell me, because I knew. He and my ma sold drugs."

"Whoa."

Doo laughed at Charlie's imitation. "Whoa!" she said. "You didn't know what you were getting into. Did you, Charlie boy?"

"Nope," Charlie admitted. "I guess I didn't."

"So!" she said sadly. "Now you know everything. You wouldn't have come if you knew, right?"

She was right, but how could he tell her that? "Sure I would," he said stoutly. "I know you're a good person."

For a minute it looked as if she was going to laugh and cry at the same time. "Well, so are you, Charlie. So are you."

19

Outside the doughnut shop, Doo suddenly said, "Gimme your hat, Charlie."

"What for?"

"Just give it to me, bro," she said. He handed it over and she set it upside-down on the sidewalk. Then she began to sing, one song after another, songs Charlie had never heard before. Sad songs, silly songs, love songs, songs about dogs and cars and just about everything anybody could dream up. People stopped to listen, but even when they didn't stop, they threw a few coins into Charlie's hat.

Charlie just watched her and listened as she sang. He thought about the girl who sang the rainbow song in the movies, and about Linda Louise Barnes, who sang opera at the John Muir talent show. Doo was just as good as them. If she knew how good she was, if she knew that she could be famous someday, maybe she'd be more careful about what she did now.

"Doo?" he said at the end of one of her songs. "Are you going to make records some day? CDs?"

"Me?" She laughed. "Nah! I could never sing in front of anybody."

"Huh? What do you think you're doing now?"

"Oh, this doesn't count," she said with a brush of her hand. "Nobody knows who I am. I could never sing on a stage or nothin'!"

Charlie just shook his head. "You *could*, Doo. You have to believe in yourself."

"Oh, Charlie, you're such a kid." She sighed.

"Oh, yeah? What about you?"

"I'm sixteen." She laughed. "Sweet sixteen. And don't you forget it!"

The lights went off in the doughnut shop, leaving Charlie, Doo, and the red cowboy hat in the darkness. "Count up what we got, Charlie," Doo said.

He bent down to retrieve his hat.

"Hey!"

Charlie turned and saw the boy named Shep. On the other side was Joel. His heart turned over.

"Hey," he said back, sounding braver than he felt.

"Hi, you guys!" said Doo, bending to help Charlie gather the coins. "Your friend Jason gave me this great idea. I got me a career now!"

"Where you guys headed?" Shep asked.

"We're just hanging out," Doo said. "How about you?"

Shep shrugged. "Hanging out."

Joel watched the money. He never said a word. He just looked out of the narrow, glittering slits of his eyes as the money disappeared into Charlie's pockets.

They began walking together, all four of them, as if they had some place to go. Shep had long, lanky legs that easily matched Doo's stride, and his ears, like Doo's, had things stuck into them. They looked like brother and sister with their light blond hair and thin pale faces. Shep had a friendly smile but his blue eyes danced nervously. "Where you guys from?"

"Up north," said Doo. "Cops got my car, though."

Why was she talking to these guys?

"Well, hey, you need a place to stay?"

"No!" shouted Charlie.

Joel said something under his breath, but Charlie didn't hear what it was.

"*Charlie!*" said Doo, sticking her fists on her hips.

"Yeah," she said to Shep. "We kind of do. For tonight, anyway. You got a place?"

"His brother's house." Joel smirked. "If you can call that a place." Joel had a runny nose but nothing to wipe it with but the back of his hand. He lurched along beside Charlie, dragging the heels of his scuffed black boots.

"Come on, Joel," said Shep. "It's not so bad. Well, it

wasn't before we trashed it. There's nothing to eat, though. We ate just about everything in the house."

"That's okay," said Doo happily. "We got some money." She and Shep were striding up ahead now, Doo telling Shep all about the little yellow Bug, *bragging* that she'd stolen a car!

"Doo," called Charlie. "What about Yolanda's?"

"Oh, come on, Charlie," Doo flung over her shoulder. "Don't worry about your stuff. We'll get it later."

"I'm not worried about my stuff! I'm—"

"What stuff?" said Joel. Like a bird-dog, he sidled up next to Charlie. "Like dope? You got some *drugs*, Charlie?" He leaned down, leering like a cartoon character.

Charlie swallowed hard, walking straight ahead with his hands in his pockets.

" 'Cause you don't wanna be selling any drugs around here, Charlie boy. People got their own territory down here. You try breaking into their territory and *zip!*" Joel sliced his hand through the air.

"Huh?" What was Joel talking about? Couldn't he see that Charlie was just a kid?

But as if Joel had read Charlie's mind, he said, " 'Course, a kid like you . . ." His voice got soft and whiny. He wiped his nose on the back of his hand. "A kid looking like you . . . The cops would never suspect a kid like you . . ."

"I don't have any drugs," said Charlie in the meanest, deepest voice he had.

"Oh, I know you *don't have any drugs*," mimicked Joel. "That's not what I was saying—"

But whatever he was saying got left behind as they all trooped into the minimart and Joel disappeared.

Charlie wandered along the candy shelf, then the shelf filled with six different kinds of potato chips, then the canned soup and beans. He wasn't hungry anymore. What he had instead of hunger was a cold, empty feeling in the pit of his stomach.

Doo had laid a lipstick and a package of Twinkies on the counter and was waiting for Charlie to pay for them. Shep had a package of cigarettes and was trying to convince the lady at the counter that he was old enough to buy them. Joel had slunk out the door. He was waiting just outside with his hands in his pockets, his pants low on his skinny hips. As people walked by, Joel's narrow eyes followed them. Then he'd look down at the ground again, his back humped and gathered around his caved-in chest.

Outside, Charlie tried to stay far from Joel, but Joel fell in beside him again. "So, like I was saying . . ."

Charlie's heart thunked.

"You guys got nowhere to go, and I could, like, fix you up with a job." He pulled a Milky Way from inside his shirt. Tore it open and dropped the wrapper on the ground. He took a bite and tried to pass it over to Charlie.

"No, thanks," Charlie said.

"You could work for the guy I work for."

Charlie wondered, if Joel had a job, why he stole candy bars. But he wasn't about to ask him.

"You wouldn't have to, like, *sell* the stuff. You could be, like, the delivery guy . . ."

"What stuff?"

"Drugs, Charlie, *drugs*," Joel said. "What d'ya think we been talking about all this time?"

"Drugs? I'm not going to sell drugs! What are you, *crazy*?"

Joel didn't like that. His fake friendliness faded right away. "Well, Mister Sunshine, how you think you're going to eat, huh? How you gonna pay, like, rent and stuff? There's worse things than drugs!"

Mister Sunshine! Charlie's jaw dropped. How did he know Charlie's mother's stupid pet name for him? "Don't call me that!" he shouted.

"Mister Sunshine." Joel smirked. "Yeah, that's you, all right. Well, you'll change your mind. All the kids act like you at first, all, like, *innocent* and stuff, but there's only a couple of ways to make it on the streets. You'll figure that out soon enough. Then you'll come begging." His glittery eyes looked Charlie up and down. "And I'll be waiting."

A shiver ran down Charlie's back and he hurried to catch up with Doo and Shep.

Hinano, said the bar, in looping pink neon lights. Shep made a sudden left turn and they all followed him through a narrow passageway between the bar and a pawnshop.

Suddenly the world went dark. There were no street-lights, no light at all except for the moon, and their four shadows loomed ahead. Charlie's breath left him. He was hollow with fear. It was the scary carnival ride all over again, only this time it was real.

20

They made their way over cracked and broken sidewalks by the light that seeped through shaded windows of rundown houses. Many houses were dark and looked as if no one had lived in them for a long time. Broken-down cars lined the curbs and trash littered the sidewalks. There was no sound except for the shuffle of their feet.

They came across an orange cat, the only living thing around. The cat watched Doo and Shep pass, then threaded itself through Charlie's ankles, nearly tripping him. It was the skinniest, saddest cat that Charlie had ever seen. "Scat!" Joel said, throwing the neck of a broken bottle at the cat. Charlie watched the cat scrabble frantically to the top of a wooden fence and drop to the other side.

As they passed a house surrounded by a high metal fence and a locked gate, a huge black dog came tearing at them across a dirt yard. He hurled himself at the fence and barked furiously until they were out of sight.

Charlie's heart was still hammering when they came to a creaking wooden bridge. He could hear water trickling beneath it and thought about trolls, how you could trick a troll by telling him about an even tastier person who was behind you on the bridge. Joel was behind him.

Farther and farther they went, down dark narrow streets and even darker alleys, Charlie's spirits sinking deeper at every turn. At first, he kept track of every landmark, every change in direction (two blocks, turn left . . . , turn right past the house with the broken chain-link fence . . .). He knew he would start to cry if he thought about the white farmhouse he'd left behind, and especially about his room, his mom with her green face and green spaghetti hair coming up the stairs to tuck him in. At another left turn that took them into an evil-smelling alley between two dark houses, Charlie realized he'd lost track, lost count of all the turns. If he took off and left Doo right this minute, if he took off and ran for all he was worth, he would never find his way back.

They came at last to a dark shabby house with a broken front walk and weeds poking up through it. Shep went around to the back and they followed. Reaching his hand carefully through a shattered window in the door, Shep let them in. When the light came on, Charlie saw that they were standing in a trashed kitchen, dirty dishes and spilled food everywhere. Spaghetti sauce from an open jar lying on its side dripped from the countertop onto a mud-smeared floor. An army of cockroaches went from the stove to the cabinet above it, back and forth. The telephone receiver was off its hook, lying in a puddle of spilled orange juice.

"Dead," said Joel, giving the receiver a kick.

"Whoa!" said Doo. "You guys been partyin' or what?"

"Pretty bad, huh?" moaned Shep. "I'm gonna clean it up before my brother comes back." He gave Doo and Charlie a quick, shy grin. "I forgot it was this bad till you guys came!" He scratched the back of his neck real hard.

"Ya just can't get good help these days!" Joel smirked.

Nobody laughed. The room was too depressing.

Shep found a bag of dried noodles in a cupboard. "Sorry, guys," he said. "There isn't anything to eat."

"That's okay," said Doo. "We just need a place to sleep, right, Charlie? You guys are just great for letting us stay here. Right, Charlie?" She gave him a poke with her bony elbow.

Charlie poked her back. His stomach ached with hunger. If he didn't eat soon, he'd get tired and weak. He wouldn't have the strength to escape, to make a plan . . . "How about if I cook up some of those noodles? We can put, I don't know, some sugar on them or something."

"Count me out on that, dude," Joel said.

Shep reached up and got the noodles. "Knock your-self out." He grinned, handing Charlie the box. Charlie scraped out a pot that had something thick and brown stuck to the bottom of it. He set the pan full of water on the stove to boil. He tried to ignore the roaches.

"Charlie's a Boy Scout," said Doo. "He can do just about anything. He has this little, like, stove? And he made us hot chocolate out in the woods? It was the coolest thing!"

Charlie stirred the noodles into the boiling water. He tried to remember what the Scout manual said about being lost.

Well, you had your compass. You could read north by looking for moss on the side of a tree. Nothing in the manual said what to do in a situation like this. Probably, if it said anything, it would say to call 911. Or don't run away from home in the first place.

When the noodles were soft, Charlie turned toward the sink. With a clutch of fear deep inside, he saw that Joel had been standing behind him all along, just standing there staring. With shaking hands, Charlie drained the water into the sink and stirred a bunch of sugar into the noodles. His stupid stomach growled. It didn't know sugar noodles from a chocolate-covered doughnut.

Shep, Charlie, and Doo sat on the floor in the living room watching *The Simpsons* and passing the pot of noodles around. There was an odor in the house that reminded Charlie of the time a possom got stuck between the walls of his parents' bedroom and died. Even with the lights on, the house was dim and shadowy.

"Hey, this is good!" said Shep, digging his fork into the pot for a second helping.

"See? I told ya what he could do!" Doo stuffed a forkful of noodles into her mouth. She smiled proudly at Charlie, as if he really *was* her brother.

"Hey, gimme some of that," demanded Joel, getting up off the couch, where he was smoking a cigarette and dropping the ashes on the floor.

"Oh, you don't want any of *this* stuff." Shep grinned at Doo and Charlie.

But Joel snatched the pot and fork away from Charlie, whose turn it was. He took a bite and made a face. "That *sucks*, man," he said and slunk back to his corner of the couch. But Charlie, lightheaded with hunger, thought it was great. If only Joel would go away. It was Joel who scared him, watching his every move, watching them all with restless red-rimmed eyes.

Doo asked Shep where his brother was.

But Shep couldn't tell her. "All's I know is that he said he was going to be gone for a while, he couldn't tell me where, and not to go near the house until he came back."

"Is he a spy or something?" asked Doo, her eyes wide.

"Nah," said Joel. "He's a dealer. Isn't he, Shep? Everybody down here deals."

Shep shrugged. "I don't know . . ." His blue eyes clouded over. "I don't know what he does."

"I'm splitting," announced Joel. "Back later. Don't you dudes do anything I wouldn't do. Ha!" He slammed out the back door and a shard of glass crashed to the floor. Charlie breathed a sigh of relief.

Once Joel was gone, a dark cloud seemed to lift off them all. They watched TV and talked about their favorite shows. That led to favorite other things. It almost felt normal to Charlie, as if they were having a good time. But how could that be, in a place like this?

"Cherry vanilla ice cream," said Doo. "On a waffle cone."

"A big fat steak!" said Shep.

Charlie, of course, said chocolate-covered cream doughnuts.

"Pink Dream eye shadow!" said Doo.

The boys turned and gave her the exact same look of disbelief.

"Sarge," said Shep.

"Who?"

"My dog."

Doo shucked her shoes and climbed up on the couch. "Where is he?"

Shep rubbed and rubbed at something on his ankle. He looked as if he was about to cry. "We had to give him away," he said. "When Mom and me got kicked out of our apartment."

"What about your brother? Couldn't he take him?"

"He wouldn't," Shep said. "He wouldn't even take Mom and me." He gave a short, hard laugh. "Says Ma's a druggie."

"Is she?" Charlie couldn't help asking.

"Yeah, I guess," said Shep. "She tries to stop but, well, I guess it's too hard for her. I want to help her, but . . ." He shrugged. "I don't know what to do."

"I know how that is," said Doo. "My mom's the same way. She keeps, like, *apologizing* every time and promising things are gonna get better. They never do."

They sat in glum silence.

Then Charlie said: "Molly the horse."

Shep and Doo looked at Charlie as if he'd gone crazy.

Charlie shrugged. "Favorite things."

And they were off again.

"Red licorice."

"Summer vacation."

"Skates."

"Brand-new kittens."

"Being six years old," said Doo. "A red bucket and a shovel on the beach . . ."

They watched a rerun of *Star Trek* and Charlie's mood went straight downhill. Never in his life had he been so homesick. Not on any of his camp-outs. He missed his folks more than he ever thought he could, and with the missing came this scary new feeling that he might never see them again. Laying his head on the arm of the couch, he closed his eyes and saw the old farmhouse exactly as he left it, with its dark windows and sleeping fields, but it looked like somebody else's house now, as if it were trying to tell him that it was no longer his.

21

Things looked a little better in the morning, the way his mom always said they would. Joel hadn't come back. Charlie hoped he was gone for good. He cooked up the rest of the noodles and they passed them around.

Nobody said how good they were this time.

Charlie sized up the dirty kitchen. "You got any big old trash bags?"

"I think I saw some around here someplace," said Shep, and began to search through the drawers.

"I'll do these yucky dishes," said Doo, making a face. "But you'll owe me for the rest of your life."

"Save the cans for Yolanda," Charlie said.

It took them most of the day to clean the house. The last thing Charlie did was to tape cardboard over the broken window. "For now," he said. "Until you can re-place it."

"Let's call out for a pizza!" said Doo.

"Great idea!" said Shep. "But no phone!"

When Charlie had hung the dead phone back in its cradle, a wave of fear had run straight through him. From the time he was little, he'd known he could always get help, no matter where he was, by dialing 911. It was a safety line to the good guys. Now the safety line had snapped.

"Thanks for all the work you done." There was a big smear of grease across Shep's forehead and another one down his arm. He was different without Joel around. He seemed like a regular kid. Charlie wondered what Joel did to make Shep so nervous, and why Shep would hang around somebody like that. Did he make Shep sell drugs?

"I couldn't have done it by myself," Shep said. "I don't think I would have tried. I start things and, like, I just can't seem to finish. You know?"

Doo said she knew. Her flowered dress was covered with spots but she looked kind of happy.

She gazed all around at the clean room. "Looks like a whole new place!"

"Thanks, guys," said Shep. He gave a high-five to Doo and then to Charlie.

The door burst open. "Hey!" yelled Joel. "What's this crap on the window?" He staggered, almost losing his balance. "What's the matter with you?" he said to the three of them, who stared as if they'd forgotten who he was. "Did ya think I wasn't coming back? I got the stuff, Shep!"

"What stuff?" said Shep warily, but he seemed to know.

"The stuff I told ya about." Joel pulled out a chair and dropped into it. He slung his head back to get the greasy dark hair out of his eyes.

"I told you no drugs in my brother's house, Joel. I mean it," Shep said. But his voice had a whine in it, and he couldn't meet Joel's narrowed eyes.

Drugs! Charlie glanced quickly at Doo, whose mouth was open, her eyes wide with surprise. They exchanged nervous looks.

"Drugs, schmugs!" said Joel. "Anyway, it's not drugs. It's natural. A *natural* high. It's good for you."

Charlie watched with cold horror as Joel reached into his pocket and took out a piece of folded tinfoil. Carefully he peeled the packet open. Inside were four capsules. With a sick, pounding heart, Charlie remembered all the times in his life he'd been warned about this exact thing, about somebody offering him drugs. He never really believed it would happen. Not to him! In the DARE class at school, he'd almost laughed at how easy it would be just to say no and walk away.

Instead, it was like a nightmare in slow motion. All he could see were the four greenish-brown capsules on the tinfoil in Joel's sweaty palm. Charlie couldn't move. He could hardly breathe.

"I told'ya I was thinking about'cha!" crowed Joel. "Four! One for each."

"Put that away, Joel," said Shep.

"*What?*" Joel stood. He made a move toward Shep. Shep backed away.

"I said, put it away," Shep muttered, blinking nervously.

"Well, if it ain't Mr. Goody-Goody. Don't let Shep here fool ya." Joel winked at Doo and Charlie. "He's the biggest druggie around. Ain't'cha, Shep? Tell the truth." He turned and laid the four capsules on the empty kitchen table in a careful row. "One for each," he said. "One for each."

Joel picked up one of the capsules. Shep hung his head, stuck his hands in his pockets. Then he slipped one hand out and reached for a capsule, too. He wouldn't look at Doo and Charlie. "C'mon, Shep," Joel said, leading him down the hall. "You guys can come, too."

22

"Let's go!" Charlie whispered when Joel and Shep were gone. "Let's get out of here!"

Doo didn't seem concerned. "It's late, Charlie," she said.

"So?"

"So, I'm tired. Let's just stay till morning. We can take turns keeping guard."

"But what about the drugs, Doo? We shouldn't *be* here."

Her eyebrows went up. "Well, I'm not gonna take that stuff, are you? Don't worry about it."

They argued back and forth, but Doo wouldn't budge. Charlie could take off if he wanted to, she said. But he didn't want to. He didn't want to go alone, and he didn't want to leave her here.

They went into the living room and sat on the floor in front of the couch and the dark television set. In the distance a dog whined and yelped, on and on. The house was quiet, no sounds in the back room. Charlie didn't want to think about what was going on there.

"How come you don't talk much about your family, Charlie?"

Charlie shrugged. "It makes me sad, I guess. Homesick."

"You feel bad that you left now, huh?"

"Yeah."

"Me, too." Doo frowned, thinking. "It felt *good* to take off like that. At first."

"Yeah . . ."

"Now it's just . . . kind of scary."

"Yeah."

Far away, a car alarm wailed.

Doo crawled across the rug and turned the TV on. But even *The X-Files* couldn't steal Charlie's mind away from what was going on in the bedroom.

"At least it's a place to stay," Doo said in the middle of an episode of *Third Rock from the Sun*. "We're not, like, sleeping on the street or nothin'. Too bad we didn't buy some popcorn. We could cook it in the microwave."

"There are drugs in the kitchen, Doo. I don't even want to go in there!"

"Relax, cuz." She laughed.

Shep burst into the room. "Something's wrong with Joel. I can't wake him up!"

Charlie and Doo scrambled to their feet. They ran down the hallway after Shep.

Joel lay curled like a shell on the floor of the bedroom. His face looked blue-gray and lifeless.

"He took two of those capsules—both his and mine," said Shep, his blue eyes darting nervously. "I don't even know what it was. He just said, *Down the hatch*, and swallowed them." He waved a shaky hand at Joel. "Is he dead? God, I hope he's not dead!"

Charlie moved by instinct. He knelt next to Joel and put two fingers on his neck in search of a pulse. Nothing. He tried again. He pried open Joel's mouth, even though he didn't much want to, and with his fingers checked inside. Then he rolled Joel over so that he was lying on his back. With his eyes closed, Joel didn't look like a jerk anymore; he just looked like a regular kid. "Get a blanket," Charlie ordered. "We've got to keep him warm."

Doo pulled a blanket off the bed and covered Joel with it.

Shep shook his head. "He said it was natural!"

"So is heroin, dummy," said Doo. "It comes from poppies. What'll we do, Charlie?" She stood up suddenly and Charlie could hear the fear in her voice when she said: "I gotta get out of here. If the cops come—"

"Call 911, Doo. Find a phone somewhere and call. Hurry!"

"Okay. But, Charlie?"

He looked up. Tears were streaming down her face, and she was shaking, holding her skinny arms around her middle. "I can't come back, Charlie. They'll find out who I am, what I did to Manny . . ."

"Just *call*, Doo!" Charlie said.

"But you have to go, too," she insisted. "They'll think it was *your* fault, Charlie. You, too, Shep. They'll think we gave Joel the drugs. Come *on*!" She pulled on Charlie's arm. "He'll be okay. We gotta go!" She had his red hat in her hand.

"We can't," said Charlie, yanking away, taking his hat. "He could die if we don't help him." Gently, he pushed Joel's chin back and, leaning over, began the breathing he'd practiced so hard and so long to earn his merit badge. Joel's mouth wasn't anything like the dummy's, but the dummy didn't breathe, and neither did Joel.

"Oh, God, Charlie!" cried Doo.

"Go!" cried Charlie between breaths.

"Come on," said Shep to Doo. "We gotta get outa here!"

Doo took a last look at Charlie, bending to breathe life into the dark-haired boy sprawled on the floor. "I'll see ya, Charlie. Okay?" Her voice broke.

Charlie didn't answer. He couldn't. He needed all his breath. He couldn't think about Doo and what would happen next. He felt Doo behind him, hesitating. Then he heard her silver shoes clacking down the hall as she raced after Shep.

In the time before he heard the first siren, Charlie thought about many things, none of them bad or even sad, none that had anything to do with what was happening with him and Joel on the floor of a stranger's bedroom in Venice Beach. He thought about his brother Tom. How he and Tom had once made applesauce. He could still smell the apples half rotting on the ground, and he could almost taste that sour applesauce again. They'd forgotten to add the sugar. He thought about Carrie bringing him camomile tea when he had the measles. She wasn't afraid to touch him, even though she'd never had the measles. She got them the following week, and they were twice as bad as his. He remembered holding Wesley when Wesley was first born. How Wesley smiled all the time in his sleep like he was the happiest baby in the whole world. He saw his dad's proud face and his mom's teary one in the front row of the John Muir auditorium as he recited all of the Gettysburg Address with only two mistakes.

He tried not to think about the fact that Joel wasn't breathing. He just kept on breathing for him. Tears rolled from Charlie's face onto Joel's until both their faces were wet and slippery.

Dou was gone for good. She wasn't coming back. In the whole world, it was just him and Joel, a kid he didn't even like, all alone.

23

He felt her standing beside him almost before he knew she was there.

"I called, Charlie," she said breathlessly. "They're on their way."

He looked up and there she was, biting her lip, a frightened look in her green eyes. "I didn't think you were coming back." Charlie wiped his mouth. Dizzy, he bent to breathe into Joel again.

"I didn't think I was either," she said in a soft, scared voice.

Then, just when Charlie thought it would never happen, Joel took a single, long, shuddering breath, then another. He coughed.

"Joel!" Doo cried.

Joel opened his eyes and looked straight at Charlie. "What's happening, dude?" He looked frightened and confused. And then he dropped away again.

Doo pulled the blanket up around Joel's shoulders. "He's breathing," she said. "He's okay now."

"I heard an ambulance," Charlie said. "Where did it go?" He got up and peered out the dark window.

"Maybe it was for somebody else," said Doo. "Charlie?"

He turned.

"Joel's okay now. We can go."

"Where's Shep?" Charlie hadn't realized until just then that Shep wasn't there, too.

"He got scared when he knew the police were coming," she said, plopping down on the bed. "I don't know where he went."

"What about you? Aren't you scared?" Keeping an eye on the rise and fall of Joel's chest, Charlie sat down next to her.

"Yeah. You?" She blinked nervously.

"Yeah, a little," he admitted. "I was more afraid of *him*." He nodded toward Joel.

"They'll send us to Juvie, Charlie," she said.

"What's that?"

"Kid jail."

"Oh." Charlie gulped.

"You sure you don't want to get out of here?"

Charlie shook his head miserably. "I can't. He seems okay now, but something could happen before the ambulance gets here. He could stop breathing again."

"But he's not . . ." Doo bit her lip. "He's not worth

. . . he's not worth going to *Juvie* for, Charlie." She chewed off a piece of her fingernail and spit it out.

Charlie shrugged.

"Is he?"

"He's a *person*," said Charlie at last.

"Well, he isn't a *good* person!"

"It doesn't matter, Doo," said Charlie. The warmth of her shoulder touching his comforted him. "Yolanda didn't ask if we were good people before she helped us, and neither did Mr. Turner when he fixed the Bug. They just helped us because they were good people themselves."

Doo thought about it for a minute. "Do you think the world is mostly full of good people, Charlie, or bad ones?"

"Mostly good ones, I think."

"I guess you could be right," she said, but she didn't sound convinced.

"You can go, Doo," Charlie said after a while. "It's okay."

"Nuh-uh," she said. "You're my brother. I gotta stick with ya."

He grinned. "I thought I was your cousin."

She blew at a lock of hair that had fallen in her eyes. "Brother, cousin, what's the difference? Anyway, you're a good person . . ."

"So are you," he said. She might have done some pretty bad things, but Doo was a good person.

"Nah . . ." she said. "Not so good."

144

"You came back," he said. "You could have just kept going."

"Well, I'm thinking," Doo said, "I mean, since this happened and all, that running away isn't . . . well, sometimes you just gotta stop, you know, and, like, face the music."

"Yeah . . ." said Charlie. It was something his father would say, face the music. He and Tom and Carrie used to laugh at their dad's weird sayings. They'd giggle behind his back after some big lecture about grades, helping their mom, or keeping their rooms clean (*tidy*, he said, and that made them laugh, too). He'd turn away and they'd try not to bust up until he left the room.

But facing the music wasn't so funny right now.

What would have happened if he hadn't run away? If he had just "hung tough"—another of his father's sayings. If they'd all just faced the music together? One thing for sure, the music wouldn't have been a siren.

It came from a long way off, a thin, high wail, and Charlie was afraid the ambulance was going somewhere else again, and that Joel would die after all. He'd checked Joel's pulse every couple of minutes. Joel didn't wake up again, but he was breathing on his own. Sleeping.

They heard the siren again, closer this time. A car, then another, screeched to a stop in front of the house and the walls were awash in red swirling light.

24

The two policemen looked so big, so blue, that they seemed to take up the whole room. One reached down and clamped a hand on Charlie's shoulder. The other grabbed Doo's arm as she headed for the door. "Just a minute, you two." The one who held Charlie spoke into his cell phone. Terrified, Charlie heard only some of the words: "juveniles, male, female . . . OD." He holstered the phone. "Okay, let's go," he said, and jerked his head toward the door.

Joel, his face half covered with a plastic oxygen mask, went past them on a stretcher, three paramedics hurrying alongside. At the curb a white ambulance with orange stripes twirled a revolving red light. The back door opened and Joel's stretcher was slid inside.

"Where are you taking us? We didn't do anything! He saved Joel's life!" Doo struggled in the officer's grip.

She kept on trying to explain things, but the officer just ignored her. Charlie couldn't say anything. The hand on his shoulder was like the vise on his dad's tool bench. He was being pushed ahead, behind Doo and the other officer.

When they got to the black-and-white police car, Charlie was told to turn his pockets inside out. When he did, out dropped his pocketknife and the money Doo had made singing in front of the doughnut shop. The officers patted them both down, as if they were carrying guns or something. Then they had to get into the back of one of the cars. Both doors closed behind them with a solid thud. Charlie found himself facing a metal grate that separated the back seat from the front. "They won't even listen!" Doo cried. "You saved Joel's life and they won't even listen!"

"Are we going to jail?" Charlie whispered, even though they were in the car by themselves. His mouth was dry and sticky. He was too terrified to cry.

Doo didn't answer him. Red light washed across her pale face, her skinny arms. The ambulance zipped off, its siren screaming.

The officers got into the car. Doors slammed, the right one, then the left. "Where are we going?" Doo said. "Where are you taking us?"

No answer.

Charlie thought about Doo's dad and wondered if she, too, was thinking how the jail felt, how cold and lonely it was. The sound of the metal gates when they closed, a final sound, as if they would never open again.

Doo grabbed Charlie's hand. "Don't worry," she said. "They'll just put us in Juvie."

Juvie! Kid jail! Charlie closed his eyes and tried to work the tears down, but it was no use. Exhausted and afraid, he clung to Doo's hand as the car whooshed through the dark, noisy streets.

They parked behind an office building, or what looked like an office building. "Out!" The two cops stood by the open doors and Charlie and Doo scooted out opposite sides of the car. They marched single-file through a revolving glass door and into a brightly lit hallway.

"Sit," the vise-grips officer ordered, pointing to a wooden bench. Charlie took off his hat and held it on his lap. The two policemen disappeared. At the end of the hallway, another officer leaned against the wall, cutting his fingernails, but Charlie could see he was keeping an eye on them.

"How . . . how long do you think we'll be in Juvie?" Charlie said. His teeth were chattering. He couldn't make them stop, no matter how hard he clenched them together.

Doo shrugged. "I dunno. Me, probably forever after what I done."

"How about me?"

"I dunno," she said. "Maybe just a couple a years."

"In here," ordered officer vise grips, sticking his stern face out a door.

Doo and Charlie got up and trooped into a room full of desks and people. Some had uniforms, some didn't. None of them gave Charlie or Doo a second look.

"This way," said a policewoman. She crooked her finger at Doo.

Doo looked back over her shoulder. "Can't he come, too?"

But officer vise grips pulled Charlie by the arm in the opposite direction.

"Charlie!" yelled Doo. Charlie turned, but the officer pushed him toward a small darkened room. Inside was a table and two chairs. In the center of the table was an ashtray overflowing with smushed cigarette butts.

"Have a seat, kid."

The room was made of cinderblocks, just like the jail that Doo's dad was in. The only windows were skinny and high above his head. Light seeped down from a buzzing fluorescent tube. It was cold. Charlie hugged his arms and tried to keep his teeth from chattering. He sat on a folding metal chair. Real live criminals had sat in the same chair, smoking their cigarettes, being tough. Charlie didn't feel very tough.

The policeman—Starnes, Charlie noticed the name on his badge for the first time—sat on the edge of the table. He began asking Charlie questions and writing answers on a form attached to a clipboard. At first, they were the usual questions—his name, his address, his birth date—but Charlie knew it wasn't going to stop there. Otherwise, they wouldn't have him in this room. This *interrogation* room. He knew from TV cop shows what went on in these rooms.

But he was just a kid! Officer Starnes knew that. He had asked him the date of his birth. Wrote it down like Charlie was, well, a regular grownup person. Or a *criminal.*

"Um, sir?" Charlie's voice squeaked out. "Can I call my folks?"

Officer Starnes didn't even look up from his clipboard. "They'll be getting a call."

Charlie pictured his father's face, the way it would change as he listened to the voice of a police officer on the other end. Maybe he wouldn't believe what they told him. Drugs? His son had nothing to do with drugs! Maybe he would just come and take Charlie away. Sue them or something!

Or maybe he'd just tell the police that Charlie should pay for his crime, whatever it was. In his family, they obeyed the law. The Bascombs were a law-abiding family. That's the way his father said it, law-abiding. Charlie hadn't thought much about the meaning of those words until now. His parents wouldn't think of breaking the law. They didn't even go over the speed limit. The more he thought about it, the closer Juvie got. Juvie was scarier even than Joel. Juvie was probably full of guys like Joel!

Officer Starnes put down his clipboard. "Where did you get the drugs, Charles?" His eyes were kind of yellowish and close together. They bore down at Charlie like the eyes of a hawk.

"They weren't my drugs, sir. Honest!"

"You take drugs all the time, Charlie, or just this once?"

"I didn't take any drugs! I never take drugs!"

"You're a *runaway*, kid. You were arrested in a house known for drug activity. And now you want me to believe you had nothing to do with any of this? Who ya trying to kid, anyway?" He slapped his clipboard on the table. Charlie jumped.

The door opened and another policeman came in. This one was older, old enough to be a grandfather. His gray mustache was twisted up at the ends like a smile.

But he wasn't smiling.

"I don't think he wants to cooperate, Pete," said Officer Starnes.

"Oh, sure he does, Starnes. You want to cooperate. Don't you, son?" Officer Pete sat next to Charlie on the other folding chair and lit up a big fat cigar. Cigar smoke floated toward the ceiling and settled there like a cloud.

"Yes, sir," Charlie said, his eyes watering. IIis teeth

chattered a little less with the older policeman. He had Santa Claus eyes, with a real twinkle in them.

"Then why don't you just tell us and get it over with, son. That's always the best way."

"Well, sure!" Charlie shrugged. He had nothing to hide.

"Where did ya get the drugs, son? Did ya buy them, or did somebody else?"

"They were—" He hesitated. In gangster movies you were a *fink* if you *ratted* on somebody, but this wasn't the movies. This was real life, and he was in trouble. "They were Joel's drugs. We, Doo and me, we don't even know him!"

"And where did this Joel—that the guy that OD'd?" He glanced up at Officer Starnes, who nodded. "Where did this Joel buy the drugs, son?"

"I don't know. He just showed up with these four capsules, these green things. I didn't even know what they were! Doo and I didn't know!"

"See?" Starnes said. "He's not going to tell us anything. Might as well book 'em, Pete."

Book 'em!

Charlie jumped up and Officer Pete pressed him back down into his chair. "I don't know, honest! I don't know where the drugs came from."

"Well, I believe you, son." Officer Pete smiled.

Charlie breathed a sigh of relief.

"Kid like you, why, you're probably a Boy Scout or something, right?" He winked.

"How did you know? I am! Scout First Class. I—" He was about to tell Officer Pete all about his merit badges, but Officer Pete put his hand on Charlie's arm to stop him and brought his face up close.

"The thing is, son, that we can't just let you off the hook. We'd *like* to, wouldn't we, Starnes?"

Officer Starnes frowned and nodded. "Yeah."

"But we can't."

Charlie's heart thudded painfully, as if it had tumbled down three flights of stairs.

"It's important that we find the pusher, you know. We've got to stop people like that from selling drugs to, well, to Boy Scouts like you. Right?"

Charlie swallowed hard and nodded. Officer Pete didn't believe he was a Boy Scout, after all. If he did, he'd know that Charlie would never do an awful thing like selling drugs. A Scout would die first.

"It's hard to squeal, I know. Sometimes they threaten you, tell you they'll hurt you or your friends . . ."

"Yeah," said Charlie.

"So, is that what they did, Charlie? Scare you into keeping your mouth shut?"

"No, sir! *Joel* got the drugs. He just showed up with them when we were cleaning the house!"

Officer Pete looked at Officer Starnes. They both shook their heads.

"Well, son," Officer Pete said. "I don't know what to tell you. You look like a pretty smart kid, but—" He shook his head and sighed, like he was very sad, like

Charlie had really let him down. "Maybe you need a little time to think about this. How about it, Starnes? How about if we give the kid a little more time before we book him?"

Officer Starnes frowned at Charlie. "You'd better do some real hard thinking, kid," he said.

25

Charlie laid his head down on his folded arms. Tears dripped from his face onto his arms and puddled on the table. He was going to Juvie. There was nothing he could do about it. He'd have a record. He'd be one of the bad kids now. No matter what he said, Officer Starnes and Officer Pete were never going to believe him.

He waited there for the longest time, so tired he nearly dropped off several times. But each time, he'd shake himself awake. He had to *think*. He had to make the police believe him. But all he really knew was what he'd told them, which was the truth.

He wondered what time it was. It felt like the middle of the night. Above his head, the light buzzed. It reminded him of the one at Four Corners Donut, how he'd sat there happily eating his chocolate-covered cream and thinking he'd be gone just one night. How he'd planned to call his folks from somewhere close, how they'd hop right in the car and come get him. How they'd be kind of mad at first, but so relieved to have him back. How they were going to tell him right away that they'd changed their minds. Charlie should never have run away, they'd have said, but he'd taught them a lesson. A painful lesson (which was the only kind his father had any use for).

But then Doo came.

Well, it wasn't her fault, all this. If only she hadn't seen her father! Up till then, she'd thought she was going to live with him. If she hadn't seen her father, they'd have stayed with Yolanda and Yolanda would have called his folks.

It was Joel. *Joel*'s fault. But Charlie, all cried out, knew better than to blame Joel, even though he wanted to. Never in his life did he want to blame somebody else so badly. But when Charlie had slipped on his backpack in his minuscule bedroom, he hadn't even known Joel. And that's the way it all began: Doo finding him at the doughnut shop, the race to the little yellow car—the little yellow *stolen* car—the breakdown, Norma and her goats, John Turner, Yolanda and her cats, Jerry Doolittle in the jail, Shep's brother's house, and then *this*. This worst, most horrible thing. It wasn't Joel's fault. Maybe Joel even learned his lesson, his *painful* lesson.

He heard the doorknob rattle and jerked his head up. "You can come out," Officer Starnes said and Charlie hurried after him.

And then he was in the hallway on the bench again, only this time by himself. Where was Doo? What did she tell them? If they didn't believe him, how would they ever believe her? She didn't even know *how* to tell the truth.

People came and went. Sometimes they glanced at him, sometimes they didn't. One lady who was young and pretty smiled at him as she passed by. She looked as if she didn't know why a kid like him would be sitting in the hallway so late at night when he should be home in bed. But she was the only one.

At the far end of the dimly lit hallway was a Coke machine and a machine that dispensed candy bars and cookies. Charlie thought about the change no longer in his pockets. The quarters, dimes, and nickels scattered all over the ground at Shep's brother's house.

He could ask to borrow some money for a candy bar. From somebody like the pretty lady, if she came out again. But how could he pay her back? How would he get the money to pay her back in Juvie?

Sick at heart, he curled up into a ball on the hard wooden bench, his hands tucked under his head. The black-and-white tiles swirled dizzily beneath him and he fell into an exhausted sleep.

"Son?" He felt his shoulder being shaken. He didn't want to wake up. He didn't want to go to school today. He was too tired. He still had the measles. "Son?"

Charlie opened his eyes. "Dad?" He sat straight up,

rubbing his eyes to wake himself up. To make sure it was his father standing there, and not some dream version of him.

"You ready to come home, son?" In his father's eyes was a look Charlie never hoped to see again in his life. He didn't even know what to call that look, there were so many different kinds of things in it. Sadness, fear, anger, and a whole lot more that would take years to know and to understand.

There was so much Charlie needed to tell his father, but all he could say was that he was ready. It wasn't enough, it wasn't nearly enough to say how glad he was to see his father again. He wanted to throw his arms around his father's neck. He wanted to laugh and cheer and punch his fist in the air. And cry. But he couldn't. It was all too much. "I'm ready, Dad," he said.

26

They'd gone around the training ring a dozen times, Wesley tucked between Charlie's legs, Molly's back gently swaying. Tom was being so patient, so unlike Tom, that Charlie could hardly believe it. He kept leading Molly around and around the ring without complaining, without saying as he always did, "This is the absolute *last* time. I've got *better* things to do than—"

But Tom had changed. It was hard to believe, but so had Carrie. When Charlie got home the day before, Carrie had been waiting on the porch. He wasn't out of the Volvo a minute when she grabbed him in a hug. "You dumb jerk." She sniffed. "You dumb jerk!"

But it wasn't Charlie's leaving that had changed things at home. It was certainly not that.

He didn't want to admit what he knew now was

true. Things had changed not because Charlie had left but because Tom and Carrie had stuck it out.

Tom, who always took off with his friends at every chance, had begun to hang around the house, doing some of the things their father always did, like burning the trash and feeding the animals. He even oiled the screen door so that it closed with a sigh instead of a shriek. Carrie did the dishes now without whining about it. She read Wesley his bedtime story as if she really enjoyed the silly story herself.

And, biggest miracle of all, they'd stopped bickering. They worked at making their mother smile again.

It wasn't fun being the bad one, the troublemaker. He had always been the good guy, the problem solver.

Mister Sunshine.

But Mister Sunshine was on probation. *Probation* was a word he didn't like. In fact, hated. A word he wanted to kick away, as if it couldn't have anything to do with him. Once a month for a whole year he and his parents would have to visit his probation officer in Fresno, where there was a juvenile hall, which is the place he would have to go if he committed a crime or ran away again. If he ever committed a *crime*, Officer Pete said when Charlie's father came to pick him up, a terrible word. But Officer Pete also said that Charlie had saved Joel Deeter's life, a pretty amazing thing for an eleven-year-old kid, and that he didn't have to. That most kids couldn't have, or wouldn't have. The probation was because he was a runaway consorting with other runaways, and because there were drugs in the house.

Well, he was through *consorting*, that was for sure.

Driving home from Los Angeles, his dad, to Charlie's surprise, hadn't said much. He drove straight up Highway 5, wearing his stone face, and when they stopped for lunch they just went straight to the drive-in and ate silently on the road. Charlie wanted his dad to yell at him and get it over with. He wanted his dad to be anything but sad.

At home, he was on restriction. Probation and restriction, a double whammy. But that was just fine with Charlie, because he couldn't think of anything he wanted more than to stay home. To hang out in his room, his own clean—well, mostly clean—room and think about how lucky he was to have all the things Doo would probably never have. Parents who loved him no matter what he did wrong, a safe home, three dogs, seven cats, Molly the horse. Even the boring fish.

His first night home, after he'd told everybody what had happened to him from the hour he walked out onto the porch and heard the wood dove calling, he prayed for the first time in a long time. Too long, he figured. Some problems were just too big for a kid to solve, even a Boy Scout with the best intentions. And Doo needed all the help she could get.

Sometimes it still surprised him a little that he couldn't get people to do the things he wanted them to, the things he thought were best, and that life went right on anyway, like a stream around a rock.

Finally, on the morning of his second day home, his dad sat him down on the porch steps for a talk. What Charlie did was very wrong, he said, not only wrong but hurtful. Worst of all is that they could have lost him for good. Runaway kids disappeared all the time, his father said, and their families never got over it. Never. Charlie listened respectfully. He said "Yes, sir" every chance he got. But a question was building up inside of him, and finally he had to ask it. He asked it as respectfully as he could. "Dad?"

"Yes, son?"

"I know what I did was wrong. I'll never do it again, I promise. But I keep thinking, when families are in trouble, shouldn't they, you know, stick together, no matter what? Hang tough? Face the music?"

His dad almost smiled. He sighed through his nose. He brushed some dust off his knee. He squinted out at the road for a long time. Then he looked long and hard at Charlie. "I wish I had an easy answer to give you, son," he said softly, "but I don't. Of course families should stick together, and we will, I promise you that. But sometimes it's real hard to choose between what's best for you and what's best for everybody else. You try to do what's right, and you can't always do that. It's hard, son, that's all I can say. And it's *real* hard to say to a son that you don't have all the answers."

They sat quietly for a while, side by side, on the old porch steps. There was something missing, and at first Charlie didn't know what it was. Then he remembered. His father wasn't going to say, "There's a lesson in that, son," and clap Charlie on the knee. That made Charlie sad in a way he didn't understand.

Every day his mom would come up with some new way to punish him, something that would make Charlie sorry, she said, that he ever left home. The dirtier the job, the more gleeful she became. He even caught her chuckling to herself, *his own mother*!

And then for no reason at all she'd grab him up and hug him so hard his breath would be squeezed right out. "Don't you *ever*," she'd say, the same thing over and over, "don't you *ever* think of doing such a thing again! You hear?"

So far he'd mucked out Molly's stall, cleaned the bathrooms, scrubbed the trash cans inside and out so that they all looked new again, weeded the weed patch that was supposed to be a flower garden, and polished every shoe in the house that could be polished.

She was still thinking of new and dirtier things. He could see it in her eyes. It was terrifying.

But he whistled his way through every job, no matter how hard, no matter how dirty.

Because he was home.

He wore his red cowboy hat all the time. It made him think about Doo singing outside Wendy's Donuts, about how happy she looked when she was singing.

On a Sunday morning three weeks after he was home again, they stopped at Four Corners Donut on the way back from church. When they were crammed into a booth and munching their doughnuts, the old man came shuffling over with an envelope in his hand. "This for you?" he said, handing the envelope to Charlie. Charlie looked at the address on the envelope. *For the kid in the red cowboy hat*, it said, followed by the name of the doughnut shop and the number of the highway, and Oakhurst, California. "Thanks," Charlie said, puzzled.

He tore open the envelope. Inside was a letter written on lined school paper.

Dear Charlie (Bro-Cuz),

I guess you are surprised to hear from me. Right? Well, I am in Juvie. Too young for jail, ha ha. It's not too bad here. At least there is stuff to eat and clean beds and all. Some of the kids are jerks but—hey—nothing new. Right? I will be here for a while, I hope not too long.

Manny is okay. All he got was a sprained ankle from running out of the house so fast, so it's mostly the car thing I'm in for. And the burned-down house.

But guess what? Yolanda comes to see me all the time. She brought me all my stuff. (She says she will take care of your backpack until you can come for it.) Did you know that she sews stuff? She makes all her clothes, that ugly parrot dress? Anyway, she made me this dress out of this yucky green stuff that is practically down to my knees. It has lace! God! I would not wear it on another planet *but what could I say?*

Anyway, if that's the worst thing then things are not too bad. Right? She says my dad will be out before I am and that we will all get a house together. She tells the truth, that is the thing I found out about Yolanda. She says we have to have rules. Just like Boy Scouts, ha ha. I guess I need some rules.

Charlie, maybe you are only thirteen years old (if you are really thirteen!) but you are pretty grownup for a kid. You didn't think twice about staying with Joel, even when you knew you could get in some real trouble. You made me think pretty hard about some things. And so when they put me in here, I didn't feel rotten or anything. I figured it was time to think about

what I am doing in my life so that I can be as
proud of myself someday as you can be right
now.

Well I probably would not say this to you in
person but I love you, Charlie. Now don't get all
weird or nothing, you know how I mean that.
Maybe we won't see each other again for a long
time but I hope you won't forget me. We had us
a time, that's for sure.

Love,
Mary Louise Doolittle (Doo)

Charlie folded the letter very carefully and put it back in its envelope. When he looked up, he saw that everybody was staring at him, even Wesley.

"Well?" said his mother.

"It's from a friend of mine," said Charlie. "It's private."

"Private? What do you mean, private? You're an eleven-year-old child."

"It's all right, Jean," said his dad. "Charlie isn't a child. Not anymore."

They pulled up in front of the old farmhouse. Their mother slid out with Wesley in her arms. Tom and Carrie got out of the backseat and headed for the house. Charlie got out the back. Then, with a wave and a smile, as if everything was just the way it was supposed to be, his dad drove off alone.